Holden has watched as many of the gargoyles in his clutch have found their mates. His hope that his own mate will turn up begins to wane when years pass, and no new mates are found by the remaining single members of the Falias clutch. He begins to despair that Fate has moved her gift of mates to another clutch.

When a fellow gargoyle's mother becomes gravely ill, the chieftain of another clutch — Chieftain Kinsey, who is also her son — comes to pay his respects. Holden is pleasantly shocked to find, amidst all the grief, there's a ray of happiness. One of the men in Chieftain Kinsey's entourage is his mate. He learns the man's name is Lathe, and he's a vampire.

Except, Holden discovers that scenting Lathe and wooing him are two very different things. Lathe only came because Chieftain Kinsey wanted his people to review Maelgwn's security measures while he was there. Holden realizes that Lathe's reclusive and wary nature has something to do with the scarring he sports on his left side.

Can Holden figure out a way to earn Lathe's trust before the one who left Lathe so scarred comes to finish what he started?

Charming his Wary Vampire
Copyright © 2022 Charlie Richards
ISBN: 978-1-4874-3536-3
Cover art by Angela Waters

Published by eXtasy Books Inc

Look for us online at:
www.eXtasybooks.com

# Charming his Wary Vampire
## A Paranormal's Love: Book Thirty-Six

By

## Charlie Richards

# CHAPTER ONE

When Lathe Mantuvian heard his phone ring, he nearly ignored it. The lines on the screen were just too captivating . . . and bone-chilling.

*He's still alive, and he's found me.*

After nearly fifty years, Lathe couldn't believe it. He rubbed his palm over his left thigh, feeling the indents and bumps where he'd lost muscle in his leg. The beating had been bad enough, but the fire . . . that had been what should have ended his life.

Only Sorbin's intervention had saved him.

The trill of his phone ringing again yanked Lathe out of his memories. He turned away from the unsettling words and focused on his phone. Seeing Sorbin's name on the screen, he happily grabbed the device and accepted the call.

"Hi."

For an instant, Sorbin didn't respond. "What's wrong?"

Grimacing, Lathe felt a tremble work through him. "I say one word, and you think something's wrong?" He rubbed his palm over his damaged leg again. "How?"

"I know you, Lathe," Sorbin replied softly. "Your tones have different qualities depending on if you're distracted, excited, or in this case, upset. So" — he pressed — "what's upset you?"

"Can you come to my office, please?" Lathe knew there was no point in denying it. Besides, he could really use his friend's advice.

"I'll be right there," Sorbin promised, then disconnected.

Lathe wished he could focus on something other than the message on his screen, but it kept snagging his attention.

*There you are, pet. I've been looking for you. And in such a nice secluded location. See you soon.*

Tears burned at the backs of Lathe's eyes, and he swiftly blinked them back. After almost fifty years, the asshole was back. It had been so long that Lathe had fallen into a false sense of security.

*There was never a body. I shouldn't have allowed myself to become complacent.*

The bang of his office door slamming against the backstop caused Lathe to jump. A squeak of alarm that he would forever deny escaped him. He swung around in his chair, pressing a palm to his chest.

Relief flooded him when he spotted Sorbin hurrying across the large computer room to reach him. Sorbin's beloved, Second Destrawn, stood inside the doorway. He peered around with a scowl darkening his features, glaring at everything.

Sorbin grabbed Lathe and hauled him to his feet. His fellow vampire wrapped him in a tight hug, clutching him close. He even rubbed a palm up and down Lathe's back, obviously catching on that he needed soothing.

Sagging into the larger vampire's hold, Lathe hugged his friend back. They stood that way for several seconds before Lathe felt someone else join them. Huge dark-green arms wrapped around both of them, telling Lathe that it was Destrawn.

A second later, a low vibrating noise not only filled the room, but it seemed to sink into Lathe's bones. He immediately felt his pulse slow, and he began to breathe easier. His body sagged a little between the two men.

"Wow," Lathe mumbled after a moment. "So that's trilling."

"That's trilling," Sorbin confirmed.

Lathe had heard of the gargoyle ability. They made a humming, vibrating noise that he'd heard was soothing. The ability was usually used to soothe an upset mate, someone injured, or when caring for a child. Lathe had never expected to experience it himself.

The tales didn't do the phenomenon justice.

"Are you settled, Lathe?" Destrawn asked, ceasing his trilling. He spoke in a soft, deep voice, betraying that he was still worried about him.

With a sad sigh, Lathe admitted, "I don't know how to answer that."

"Start by telling us what upset you," Sorbin encouraged, squeezing his shoulder. He began releasing Lathe, so Destrawn did the same, obviously catching his cues from his lover. Sorbin peered down at Lathe and offered him an encouraging smile. "Whatever it is, we'll fix it."

Shaking his head, Lathe murmured, "I'm not sure you can." Before his friend could counter him, he pointed at his computer screen. "I received that thirty minutes ago."

Sorbin read the message, and a frown immediately creased his brows. A low growl escaped him. "And you're assuming that's from Edward?"

Lathe cringed just from hearing the vampire's name. "Yeah."

"Who's Edward?" Destrawn asked, sounding a mixture of confused and concerned. "No one good, I take it."

Sneering, Sorbin stated, "Edward's a rogue. We were told he'd been put down."

"The long and the short of it is" — Lathe inhaled deeply, focusing on Destrawn as he tucked his long hair behind his left ear, revealing the extensive scarring on his cheek and trailing down his neck — "he kidnapped me when I was out clubbing. He called me his pet and tried to turn me into his submissive." Crossing his arms, hugging his torso, Lathe told him, "He

3

beat me, extensively, when I refused. I was unconscious when the house he'd been squatting in caught on fire." Focusing on the floor, Lathe muttered, "Sorbin found me and saved me. He found us a new coven. That's how we ended up out here."

"Why?" Destrawn asked. "Not that I don't appreciate that you ended up here."

"We were in a coven in Montgomery, Alabama at the time," Sorbin shared. "Very conservative, and Lathe was open about the fact that he preferred men." A low growl filled his voice as he stated, "When I told the master that Lathe was missing, he said, *good*, and refused to assign enforcers to help me find him."

"Asshole," Destrawn snarled. "Those types of leaders should be taken out."

Sorbin chuckled coldly. "Oh, he was. I reported him to the Vampire Council."

Recalling those days, Lathe shivered. Once again, both Sorbin and Destrawn wrapped their arms around him. He sighed as he soaked up the comfort. Lathe wasn't a fan of being touched, but right then, he knew it was exactly what he needed.

"Anyway," Lathe cut in, needing to move the story along. "The Vampire Council assigned a pair of enforcers to the case. They were supposed to track him down and take him out. Eventually, I received word that he'd been dispatched. But when I asked to see the body, I was told that he'd died in a fire and the body had already been disposed of." Grimacing, Lathe admitted, "At the time, I'd thought it poetic justice."

"But you think that message is from Edward, and he's still alive?" Destrawn mused.

"Yeah." Frowning, Lathe mumbled, "But I have no idea how it could be. He's supposed to be dead."

"And you don't think it's someone else messing with you?"

Sorbin growled upon hearing his beloved's question. "Not

a chance," he declared. "No one but me knew about the pet thing, and I sure as hell would never send something like that."

"Well, then it's a good thing you'll be away from the clutch for a while," Destrawn stated, confusing Lathe. "Plus, I hear the Falias clutch has a couple of kick-ass hackers. Maybe they can help you figure out where this message came from."

Confusion flooded Lathe. "I'm sorry. What?"

*What is the second talking about?*

"Oh, sorry," Sorbin answered. "That was originally why I was calling. Chieftain Kinsey needs to go to the Falias clutch in Colorado. His brother, Conchlin, contacted him." Sorbin grimaced and shook his head. "Their mother lives there, Wendy, and her health is failing. Their doctors are doing what they can, but with the death of her gargoyle mate, even with their link as strained as it had been, they don't think Wendy has too much longer to live."

"It's impressive that she outlasted him by a couple of years as it is," Destrawn pointed out with a grimace. "But she's already lived almost four hundred years, and it sounds like she's ready to move on to the next life."

"Wow, I'm sorry to hear that," Lathe murmured, feeling sorry for Conchlin. He'd heard how he'd been estranged from his family for over a century due to the bigotry of the chieftain who'd been in charge before being rousted by Chieftain Kinsey. *Still* – "Um, what does that have to do with me? Why would *I* go with them?"

"They'd like you to work with their IT guy, Raymond, and review the security measures for both us and them," Destrawn explained. "I guess they have a really great set-up, and Kinsey wants to know if they can offer insight on improving our own. Plus, fresh eyes for them sort of thing."

Lathe nodded slowly even as he mentally cringed at the idea of traveling to a strange clutch. "Guess because the chieftain is going, that means you won't be going, huh?" He met

Sorbin's gaze. The other vampire was more a brother than a friend, and Lathe knew he relied on him probably a little more than he should.

"Afraid not," Sorbin confirmed, his expression rueful. "With the chieftain gone, Destrawn will be in charge, and—"

"Your place is by his side," Lathe finished for him, scoffing softly. "I knew that even before I asked." Easing out of both men's holds, he felt grateful that Sorbin had ended up with such an understanding beloved who didn't mind that he hugged Lathe. "So, uh, when do we leave?"

"Chieftain Kinsey and Jimmy want to fly out as soon as night falls," Destrawn told him. "He'll be carrying his mate, and you'll be carried by Sethnos."

Lathe grimaced, even as he nodded. It wasn't the fact that Sethnos—the clutch's head enforcer—was carrying him. It was the fact that he had to fly at all.

"It's the quickest way," Destrawn stated, obviously catching on to his unease. "Don't worry. Sethnos will take good care of you."

"I just like having my feet on the ground," Lathe admitted with a shrug. Seeing the concern in Sorbin's eyes, he quickly added, "I'll deal. If the chieftain wants me to go, I'm honored to go."

Lathe was, too. As much as he enjoyed staying behind the scenes with his computers, he still appreciated being useful to his coven . . . or clutch, as it were. Lathe had only been with the gargoyles for a few months, and he was still getting used to their terminology.

"Then head out and pack," Sorbin encouraged, squeezing Lathe's shoulder. "Tracker Dwayne and Enforcer Lakota will be accompanying you all, and they'll be carrying everyone's stuff, so pack light."

"Can I carry my laptop bag myself?" Lathe asked, turning toward the mentioned item and beginning to close his files.

"If I'm going to be working with Raymond, then I'll want to have it with me."

Destrawn nodded. "I'm certain that won't be an issue."

Sorbin eased onto his office chair. "And I'm going to forward this message to Ninevah," he stated, referring to a tech guy at their old coven run by Master Krispin Stearling, who was mated to one of Kinsey's gargoyles. "Between you, him, Raymond, and whoever else is tech-savvy at the Falias clutch, we'll track this bastard down."

Lathe truly didn't want to think about it, but he knew he couldn't bury his head in the sand. "Thanks, Sorbin." If they didn't find Edward, he knew that eventually, Edward would find him. Either that or he would become a prisoner within the clutch mansion. Smiling tightly, Lathe added, "And I'll keep you in the loop."

While Lathe didn't go out often, he did like to at least have the option. He could only tolerate bagged blood for so long before he longed for some straight from the source. While Lathe hated that, due to his scars, he usually had to use his vampiric trancing abilities to secure a donor, his desire for fresh blood overrode his reticence.

"Guess I better drink a couple bags of blood while packing," Lathe mused, sliding his laptop into his bag. Trying for levity, he quipped, "I'm sure Chieftain Maelgwn doesn't want me trying to feed from his gargoyles."

"Most of those in his clutch are mated," Destrawn told him with a shrug. "So, yeah. Trying to trance them for blood would be a bad thing."

Lathe hummed as he nodded. After slinging the strap of his laptop bag over his right shoulder, he turned toward the door. Before exiting, he flicked his hair from behind his ear, doing his best to obscure his scars.

"You don't need to do that, you know," Destrawn commented softly, resting his hand on his shoulder. "No one here would think less of you." Then he shrugged and indicated his hulking frame. "After all, we look like this."

Smiling up at Destrawn, Lathe took in the big man's swarthy, deep-green hide, his massive black wings and claws, and square-jawed features with prominent canines. "Gargoyles are a handsome species," Lathe told him. "Never let anyone tell you otherwise."

"Just as your scars tell a tale of strength of will and a courageous spirit," Destrawn countered with another squeeze to his shoulder. "I'll let Kinsey know you'll be ready."

Lathe smiled and nodded before leaving the space. Glancing back, he spotted Sorbin giving Destrawn a loving smile. The way the huge gargoyle's countenance softened, expressing his love for Sorbin with just that one look, caused a pang of longing in the vicinity of Lathe's heart. He would love to have someone stare at him that way.

Limping through the large estate, Lathe shook his head. He couldn't imagine finding that type of relationship now. Back before he'd been targeted, it had been a constant dream—finding his beloved. Now, he rarely touched his scars, and he didn't like the idea of anyone else touching them either.

Lathe had actually felt a bit of relief that he hadn't ended up with a gargoyle mate like Sorbin had.

*But now I'm headed to a completely new clutch. Gods, Fate wouldn't do that to me, would she?*

Recalling Destrawn warn him that most of the gargoyles there were already mated, Lathe dismissed the idea and focused on the task at hand—getting ready to go.

*Don't want to hold up Chieftain Kinsey.*

# CHAPTER TWO

"Hey, Holden?"

Holden lifted his attention from where he'd been folding the laundry. He'd just pulled a load of towels out of the dryer, and he knew he had three more. Even with the half a dozen industrial-sized washing machines and dryers, there always seemed to be more laundry to do. It had gotten even worse after so many gargoyles had found their mates.

*Maybe I'll find mine someday soon, too.*

While the rash of mates seemed to have dwindled over the years, Holden still held out hope.

Spotting Sapian coming toward him, Holden smiled at the golden-hided gargoyle. "Yes, Enforcer?" he answered respectfully. "Need towels?" Recalling that Sapian's mate, Missy, had given birth to a baby girl several months before, Holden added, "Do you have a load of baby clothes for me?"

While working in the laundry room wasn't the most prestigious job, Holden didn't mind it. He knew it needed to be done, and he enjoyed being helpful. Besides, it kept him out of the kitchen, for which he was grateful. Holden could burn water, and Roman—their clutch's head chef—had stuck him on dish duty as punishment more than once.

Sapian shook his head. "No on the towels, but thanks, Holden." He paused and rested his hip on a bar used to fold laundry. "There are six representatives from the Aerasceatle clutch on their way, and since Karen headed off to college, we're a smidge short-handed in the housekeeping department. Can I get you to put clean sheets in a couple of rooms?"

"Sure can," Holden replied immediately. "What rooms, and should I do it right away or after I've folded these last three loads?"

Holden knew Karen was the daughter of Brogan and Katie. She'd been chomping at the bit to get out from under Brogan's eye, having been testing the boundaries for a couple of years. Holden didn't envy his fellow gargoyle the stress he must be feeling upon having Karen at college.

"They'll need fresh towels, too, so after those loads is fine," Sapian told him. "They're expected within the next hour, but I bet Chieftain Kinsey and Jimmy are going to want to see Wendy first thing." His tone turned sad as he shook his head. "It's been hard watching Conchlin's mother go downhill, but considering how long she's lived and how her mate ended up being put down, we knew it was coming."

Grimacing, Holden nodded. He'd heard the stories. Wendy had been the fated mate of a gargoyle named Creasis. Creasis had ended up listening to too many twisted lies from Chieftain Grecian, and he'd lost faith in the mate-bond.

At least, Wendy had had a few years reconnecting with Conchlin before her health began failing.

"Here's a list of the five rooms we need set up." Sapian placed a folder on the table. "When you're ready, grab Tasker from the kitchen. He can help."

Holden nodded even as he fought back a wince. He must have failed, for Sapian arched a brow and asked, "Is there a problem with you two working together?"

Quickly shaking his head, Holden returned to folding towels as he admitted, "Not a problem per se." He felt his cheeks begin to heat and appreciated his deep purple hide. "I, uh, I may have fucked Tasker a few times, and now he thinks every time we're alone together, we should fuck, and he kinda gropes me and stuff." With a sigh, Holden rolled his eyes.

"He's a little, um, distracting to work with, all things considered."

Sapian groaned as he tipped his head back. "Damn. I'm sorry," he mumbled. Cocking his head, he asked, "Is Tasker's attentions welcome, just in-opportune? Or does the inner circle need to get involved to have him cut it out?"

Shrugging, Holden admitted, "I don't mind fucking. We all need stress-relief every now and again." He saw the way Sapian smirked and knew the mated gargoyle understood. Paranormals had a pretty high sex drive, to begin with, but after mating, a couple seemed to become even hornier, or so it certainly seemed to him. "Anyway," Holden continued. "Before or after shift is fine. But I just wish he didn't try to proposition me while we're working."

Nodding, Sapian asked, "Have you told Tasker that?"

"Yeah, but I'll tell him again if he tries something while we're setting up the rooms," Holden assured. "If he doesn't listen, then I'll let you know."

Sapian nodded. "Sounds good." After patting Holden on the upper arm, the enforcer started toward the door. "And, yes, stress-relief is a good thing," he called over his shoulder. "As long as it doesn't interfere with your duties."

Holden nodded, completely agreeing. "Yes, Enforcer." He tapped the folder. "I'll get this taken care of shortly."

"Thanks, Holden." Then Sapian was gone.

After Holden finished folding the towels, he grabbed a trolley. He double-checked how many rooms he needed to make up—five—and realized he needed twenty towels—four per room. Once he'd stacked a dozen towels on the trolley, he moved to a dryer and opened it. Taking those towels to the folding table, Holden worked through them.

Holden filled the trolley with twenty towels as well as ten wash clothes and hand towels. Then he grabbed a second trolley and headed to a massive storage closet. From there, he pulled ten sets of sheets, pillows, and pillowcases, placing them on the second trolley.

After moving the wet clothes from the washing machines into the dryers, Holden put away the unneeded towels. Then he pushed one trolley in front of him while pulling the second behind him. He made his way out of the huge laundry room and over to the freight elevator.

Leaving the trolleys in the hall, Holden hurried down to the kitchen. He stepped inside, immediately feeling the heat from the ovens. After a quick look around, he spotted Tasker.

The slender gargoyle's six-foot-one frame stood at a prep table where he was dicing potatoes into fries. His pale-blue tail swung rhythmically as he shimmied his hips. He had a pair of earbuds in his ears, and it was obvious that he listened to some tunes as he worked.

Holden found his attention drifting to the gargoyle's lean hips as he shimmied, and he recalled how it felt to drive into the man's tight ass over and over. When he felt a fissure of heat coil in his gut, he yanked his gaze away from the enticing sight.

*Yep. There's a reason I've fucked him a few times. He's hot.*

As if knowing that someone watched him, Tasker paused in his work and glanced around. When he pinned his green-eyed gaze on Holden, he grinned broadly. Putting down his knife, Tasker popped his earbuds out of his ears.

"Hey, Holden," Tasker greeted. "Ready to get to work making up those rooms?" Tasker's voice practically dripped with innuendo, and his expression grew heavy-lidded. "Roman already knows I'll be stepping away for a while." He indicated the prep table with one white-clawed hand. "That's why he has me doing this busywork."

Clamping tightly onto his libido—*now so isn't the time*—Holden nodded. "Yeah. We need to work quickly," he stated, subtly reminding Tasker that they were doing a job together.

Holden even pointed at the wall clock. "According to Enforcer Sapian, the delegation from the Aerasceatle clutch should be here in less than thirty minutes."

Tasker nodded once. "Of course." He crossed to the sink and placed his knife inside before washing his hands, saying over his shoulder, "Hand me that towel, would ya?"

Relief filled Holden, thinking Tasker was actually going to be focused on their work. He spotted the hand towel Tasker indicated with his chin. Grabbing it off the rack, Holden held it out to the other gargoyle.

Before Holden could release it, Tasker tugged, urging him a step forward. A playful smirk curved the slightly shorter gargoyle's blue lips. "Plenty of time to set up five rooms." He waggled his dark eyebrow ridges as he lowered his voice to a husky drawl, "And maybe put one of them to good use beforehand."

"Oh, good grief, Tasker," Holden grumbled, shaking his head. He took a step backward while pivoting. With a growl as he stalked out of the kitchen, he muttered, "Do you have any idea what bad form it would be to offer a room smelling of sex to the delegate of another clutch?"

To Holden's surprise, Tasker scoffed derisively before saying, "Oh, come on. It's just Conchlin's brother and a few of his peeps."

Scowling at Tasker, Holden couldn't help but point out, "And Conchlin's brother is still Chieftain of his clutch." He shook his head as he watched Tasker roll his eyes. "You'd better not let Chieftain Maelgwn or any of the other inner circle hear you talking like that." Arriving at the freight elevator, Holden hit the up button, having verified that the rooms were on the second floor. Unable to help it, he warned, "You'll get more than just a smack on the wrist."

"I ain't on stupid pills," Tasker stated with a roll of his eyes.

Holden thought that was debatable, judging by his foolish

comments.

*Guess he's more beauty than brains. How did I never notice that before?*

Keeping that thought to himself, Holden pushed one of the trolleys into the elevator.

Tasker followed with the second one. As soon as the doors began to close, he stepped close to Holden, resting his palm on his abdominals and rubbing. The scrape of Tasker's claws across Holden's flesh created a predictable tingle through his belly. At the same time, Tasker placed his other hand on Holden's hip, sliding his thumb under the top of Holden's loincloth and into the V-groove of his abdominals.

Hissing, Holden grabbed both of Tasker's wrists. Ignoring the way his arousal surged, he removed the other gargoyle's hands from his body. Seeing the other male's furrowed eyebrow ridges and the twist of annoyance on his blue lips, Holden sighed deeply as he shook his head.

"Not now, Tasker," Holden stated firmly. He released the other gargoyle's wrists while deftly moving around the trolley. "We're on shift. We're working."

Tasker huffed a sigh while scowling at him. "You're no fun." They reached their floor, and fortunately, he moved to grab the second trolley. As Holden led the way out of the car, Tasker grumbled, "You know, there's only, like, five unmated gargoyles here. Everyone else has fuck-fests, putting off loads of hormones. Can you blame me for being horny all the time?"

Holden glanced over his shoulder as a flutter of unease entered his gut. "Is that why you always come onto me?"

Shrugging, Tasker replied, "Sure. I'm a switch, so when I want to fuck, I go to Twilden or Beldrew." He referred to a couple of small gargoyles who were also still unmated. Then Tasker added, "And Grimley has made it clear that he wants nothing to do with me." With a sneer and sounding outraged, he cried, "Can you believe he called me a slut?"

Biting his tongue, Holden processed Tasker's words.

"Well, I appreciate that you're not trying to get serious with me," he decided on. He'd actually been a little worried about that. "And I like to fuck as well as the next paranormal, but I'm not going to do it with you on the clock. Got it?"

Tasker sighed deeply even as he rolled his eyes. "Fine." Then his expression turned sly as he added, "But after we're done, it wouldn't hurt to take our breaks." Reaching over from where he pushed the second trolley next to Holden, Tasker rubbed his palm down his flank. "I know you must have one coming up soon."

Holden fought his urge to roll his eyes. The gargoyle really did have a one-track mind. There was sort of something to Grimley calling the guy a slut. Also, Holden couldn't imagine approaching the huge, midnight black gargoyle for anything. The only reason Grimley wasn't an enforcer was because he was reclusive as hell, wanting nothing to do with anyone other than the chieftain, second, and head enforcer. Grimley lived in a small cottage on the south edge of the property, monitoring that border.

On the other hand, Holden understood why Tasker was perpetually horny. All the mated couples really were pumping out a shit-ton of hormones. Still, Holden smacked Tasker's hand away from his ass.

"Focus on the job, damn it," Holden grumbled. "I don't need to be uncomfortable the whole time I'm tucking in sheets."

Tasker chuckled huskily. "Well, I'll be in the same boat," he told him with a brow-ridge waggle. "Guess we better hurry."

"I already said we needed to hurry," Holden muttered under his breath as he stopped at the first door. Although, to be fair, Holden wanted to hurry because he wanted all the rooms to be ready before the delegation arrived. "What do you want? Bedroom or bathroom?"

"Bedroom," Tasker rumbled suggestively.

Rolling his eyes, Holden figured he'd walked into that one. Once inside the suite, he left the trolley he'd been pushing, since it held the linens. He maneuvered around Tasker, avoiding his stroking hands, and grabbed that trolley.

Then Holden headed into the bathroom.

To Holden's surprise, Tasker seemed to remain focused on his work. Between the pair, they finished all five rooms in under twenty minutes. He was just rolling the trolley out of the final bathroom when he heard voices from the hallway.

At the same time, Holden heard Tasker call, "Hey, Holden. Can I get a hand, please?"

Knowing they needed to hurry, Holden hurried into the final room's bedroom. "What do you—Fuck," he snapped, freezing a few steps inside the room.

Holden gaped as he took in the sight of a naked Tasker sprawled out on the bed. The blue gargoyle had his hand wrapped around his erection, and he jacked himself slowly. He'd tucked his other arm under his head, and he peered up at him lustfully.

"Yep, that's the plan," Tasker crooned, slipping his hand down to cup his balls. "I'm sure we have time to do just that."

"What the hell is going on in here?"

Upon hearing Second Tobias's angry voice from behind him, Holden spun, lifting his hands in placation. "This isn't what it looks like," he sputtered, staring at those behind him. Along with Second Tobias was Enforcer Einan and a slender male who stared at him with wide, gorgeous green eyes. "I had no intention of—"

Then the scent of the stranger teased his nostrils—something light and earthy with pine undertones. His gut clenched, and his mouth watered. Arousal flooded his veins, and he gaped, almost drooling, as he took in the stranger before him.

The man's black hair was shaved scalp-close on his right side, while hanging long on his left, hiding part of his face and eye. Holden's fingers twitched with his desire to step forward and tuck the man's hair behind his ear. He wanted to cradle his jaw and wrap the significantly smaller man in his arms.

"Holy shit," Holden whispered as the realization hit him like a bolt of lightning. This man was his mate. "You're stunning."

The guy frowned even as he took a step backward. He glanced beyond Holden and swallowed so hard his Adam's apple bobbed. Shaking his head, hurt and confusion perfuming the air, the man turned away from him, clutching at the strap of his laptop case.

"I-I'd like to see Raymond, please," the man whispered softly.

"Of course," Enforcer Einan rumbled, casting a frown Holden's way. "While you're with him, I'll have a new room prepared for you."

"Thank you." Then the stranger began limping from the room.

"Wait," Holden began, stepping forward.

Except, Second Tobias clamped a hand on his shoulder, stopping him. "You're coming with me," he growled, his anger perfuming the air. Then he ordered, "Get your fucking loincloth back on, Tasker. I don't know what the hell either of you were thinking, but you'll be explaining yourselves to Chieftain Maelgwn."

Holden wanted to counter Tobias, but he knew better. It'd been a long time since he'd been on the receiving end of the second's ire. All he could do was watch his mate limp — *gods, my mate is injured* — away from him.

*Gods, I'll beg any mercy from my chieftain so I can fix this mess.*

# CHAPTER THREE

"I want to offer my sincerest apologies for that little display back there," Enforcer Einan rumbled, shaking his head. "In truth, I can't even begin to explain what the hell those two were thinking."

Lathe did his best to hide his . . . everything. His gut felt tight, and he could barely take in a full breath. He barely resisted rubbing at his chest.

Instead, Lathe focused on taking one step after another. He knew he limped heavier than usual. Flying while tucked in a gargoyle's arms for hours on end—the chill of the air all around him—had stiffened him up beyond anything he'd experienced in . . . well, it'd been decades. Of course, that was probably because Lathe had been fastidious about always working out his hip, thigh, and knee on an hourly basis.

Lathe set an alarm on his phone for it.

Unfortunately, flying while curled up in Sethnos's arms, Lathe had turned off his alarms.

Staying in one position had totally sucked.

"Really," Einan continued, sounding truly frustrated. "Please, accept my apologies. We would never purposefully insult anyone from another clutch that way . . . gargoyle or not."

"I think . . ." Lathe began slowly, deciding to take in the scene from an unbiased gaze. "I think your purple gargoyle—"

"Holden," Einan cut in, glancing his way. "The purple gargoyle is Holden. The blue one is Tasker."

Lathe grunted softly, acknowledging Einan's comment. He really didn't give a shit who the blue slut on the bed had been. Looking back on the scene, it had been damn obvious that the purple gargoyle—Holden—had been beyond shocked by the blue one's behavior—Tasker. Lathe had only been half-listening to Second Tobias's spiel about being welcome to the clutch and having the run of the grounds and all that shit.

*Okay, probably not my finest moment to be ignoring the second, but now my distraction makes sense.*

Evidently, that gargoyle—Holden—had been one of the guys preparing their rooms. His scent had saturated the hallways and rooms as each of the others had been shown to their rooms. Lathe had been confused as hell as to why the gargoyles hadn't commented on the delicious aroma filling the area. After all, they had loads more sensory receptors than a vampire did, and he could smell it.

*Sadly, now I'm pretty sure it makes sense.*

"Lathe, please," Enforcer Einan rumbled, pausing in the hallway to face him. "I really am sorry. Please, don't let a couple of idiots' actions screw up the diplomacy we have between our two clutches."

Lathe scoffed and forced a smile. "No, I won't," he assured. "You misunderstand me." Lifting his left hand, palm out in placation, he told the enforcer, "What I was thinking was . . . I think Holden was just as shocked at that blue guy's behavior." Lathe couldn't remember the moron's name, even though he'd just been told it. "I think he was starting to yell at him." Grimacing, Lathe mumbled, "Not that I wanted to see that, but I don't actually think it was the purple guy's, um, Holden's fault . . . or idea."

*Good gods, am I actually defending my beloved when I don't even know the first thing about him?*

*Guess so . . .*

Glancing toward Einan, Lathe wondered what the big gray enforcer was thinking. His head was cocked to the side as he continued down the hallway, and his eyes were narrowed. He seemed a little lost in thought.

Clearing his throat, Lathe added, "But I'd like a new room, please." He tightened his hold on his laptop bag strap. "I don't want to remember that blue asshole spread on my bed every time I try to go to sleep." Scoffing, he muttered, "I'd rather sleep on that nice sofa in the front room."

"You won't need to do that," Einan instantly assured. Glancing at him, maybe noticing the way he limped, he slowed his gait. "And now that I think about the conflicting scents in the room, I think you're probably right. Holden didn't seem too pleased with Tasker's behavior." Narrowing his eyes, he glanced Lathe's way. "Out of curiosity, how did you pick up on it?"

Swallowing hard, Lathe tried to decide on the best way to answer — something truthful but words that didn't reveal his possible connection to Holden. "Um, his shock. I could scent his shock," he murmured. With a roll of his eyes, he added, "Yes, there was a hint of arousal, but only for an instant. Then he realized what the hell was happening, and all he scented of was . . . embarrassment."

"Until — " Einan pressed. He paused outside a door and pinned a narrow-eyed gaze on Lathe. "Until he scented you."

Lathe realized there was no point in trying to hide it. Not from paranormals, after all. "Yeah. Me." Clutching his bag strap close, he mumbled, "He might be my beloved."

"Might be?" Einan absently used his knuckles to rap on the door beside him. "Because I'm pretty sure that look of shock on Holden's face says he thinks you're his mate."

Sighing again, Lathe grimaced. "Well, I'm a vampire. His blood calls to me, but I'd need to taste it to be one-hundred percent certain," he hedged, even though no other's blood had ever smelled so delicious. He knew that was an indicator, and he knew he wouldn't be able to deny him, either, no matter how uncomfortable he felt about it. "But, yeah, I'm pretty sure."

The sound of a guy calling, "Come in," interrupted them.

Einan hummed as he opened the door. "Well, Holden is a good guy. Does housekeeping and seems to enjoy it." He led the way into a large computer room with one wall covered in half a dozen monitors. "I know Sapian pulled him from laundry to take care of everyone's rooms." Shaking his head, Einan muttered, "Guess he should have chosen someone other than Tasker to help him." Then he turned his attention to the small black gargoyle seated before the monitors. "Hi, Raymond. This is Lathe. He's interested in reviewing our security to see if there's a way to boost his own clutch's safety."

"Hey, Enforcer Einan." Raymond rose from his chair and held out his hand. "Hi, Lathe. Happy to help."

Lathe shook Raymond's hand, then returned his grip to his laptop strap. "Thanks."

"I'm going to go talk to Maelgwn," Einan told him. "Talk to him about a room." Pausing near the door, he added, "Unless we should just assume you're going to stay in Holden's?"

Quickly shaking his head, Lathe replied, "I'm not comfortable with that idea."

Einan grinned. "Well, if he's pegged you as his mate, he'll try to change your mind." Then the enforcer headed out, closing the door behind him.

"Hey." Raymond grinned broadly. "Holden is your mate? That's fantastic." Grabbing a second chair and pulling it close, he continued, "I know he was disappointed when the slew of mates showing up slowed. I bet he's ecstatic." Raymond settled back in his chair as he drew his eyebrow ridges together. "Where is he, anyway?"

"Uh, I-I don't know." Lathe eased onto the offered chair,

relieved to be off his leg. "Can we just focus on work?" Resting his laptop bag on his good leg, Lathe asked, "Is there somewhere I can set up my laptop?"

Raymond eyed him for a few seconds, looking as if he wanted to ask more questions. Finally, he nodded and stood again. He crossed to a large storage cabinet and opened the door. From within, Raymond retrieved a TV tray, which he set up before Lathe.

"Here ya go," Raymond stated needlessly. "Where would you like to start?"

Appreciating Raymond's willingness to shift gears, Lathe began setting up his laptop, so they could focus on work.

An hour later, Lathe shut down his laptop. The security at the Falias clutch was top-notch, and Raymond had been able to point out a couple of vulnerable areas in the Aerasceatle clutch. After that, Raymond had set up an algorithm to search for Edward's whereabouts.

Now, all they could do was wait.

To that end, Lathe needed to stretch his leg. "Can you point me in the direction of the gardens?" He'd heard good things about it.

"I'll show you the way," Raymond offered, rising from his chair.

Lathe would have preferred to be alone, but he smiled and nodded anyway. "Thank you."

"I'll show you your new room, too," Raymond offered. He'd received a call from Einan a short while before. "It's a couple of doors down from the other room."

Nodding again, Lathe repeated, "Thank you."

Raymond smiled, leading the way. Being a smaller gargoyle, the black male stood the same height as Lathe's five-foot-ten, but his legs were shorter. That meant Lathe didn't have quite the same issue of keeping up with him as when he'd been walking with Einan, even though Lathe had noticed the large gargoyle had shortened his stride.

As they walked, Raymond asked, "So, do you think you're going to move here?"

Frowning, Lathe glanced his way. "Move here? Why?"

"Well, Holden is part of this clutch," Raymond pointed out. "He's been here for centuries."

"Right," Lathe mused. "Gotta pick a clutch." He rubbed the back of his neck with discomfort. "I just switched from a coven. I don't—I don't want to move again."

Raymond grinned at him. "Well, I figure Holden wouldn't mind a change, especially for his mate."

Lathe sighed before muttering, "Guess that sort of makes me an ass."

"Not really," Raymond countered with a smile, sounding way too perky. "Just means you feel safe there. Considering Sorbin's there, I understand." He patted Lathe on the shoulder. "I'm sure Holden will understand, too."

Nodding once, Lathe remained quiet. He'd needed to explain a little about his past when sharing his Edward problem. That included telling Raymond about Sorbin being like a brother to him.

"Okay, here's your new room," Raymond told him, stopping at a door and opening it. "Your card key is inside." He pointed at the end table.

Lathe entered, seeing that the space appeared extremely similar to the prior one. The only big difference was the scents. He didn't recognize the smell of whoever had made up the room, but it definitely hadn't been Holden or Tasker. After placing his laptop bag on a chair, Lathe returned to the door, grabbing the key along the way.

After locking the door, Lathe closed it.

"Ready for the garden?"

Lathe nodded.

They returned to the estate's main stairwell, and Lathe slowly limped down it. Raymond led the way across the foyer to a side hall. Upon reaching the door at the end, he opened it and stepped outside.

Following, Lathe realized he should have grabbed a coat.

"Oh, you're not dressed for this weather," Raymond commented. "Let me get you a coat."

Before Lathe could comment, Raymond popped back into the estate. He must not have needed to go far, for he returned momentarily with a long, thick trench coat. After helping Lathe into it, he pointed across the deck and to the right.

"The gardens are beautiful, even at night."

"Thank you," Lathe murmured, forcing a smile. "For the directions and the coat."

Raymond nodded with another perky grin before heading back inside.

Lathe let out a long sigh before limping his way across the deck. Gripping the railing, he made his way down the pair of steps. Choosing an entrance, Lathe made his way into the gardens. Instantly, he was surrounded by fragrant blooms.

Raymond hadn't been kidding. Even at night, the place was beautiful.

Strolling slowly, Lathe took his time. He didn't know the layout and enjoyed exploring. Every few moments, he stopped to stretch, working the kinks out of his left side . . . as much as he could, anyway.

Lathe allowed his mind to drift, doing his best not to focus on . . . anything.

The ringing of his phone drew Lathe's attention, and he pulled it from his inside pocket. Seeing Sorbin's name, he accepted the call. "Hi."

"Shit, Lathe," Sorbin grumbled in lieu of a greeting. "What happened?"

Snorting, Lathe rolled his eyes. "Again. One word, and you

know I'm upset." He paused at a bench near a fountain and sat down. "I still don't know how you do that," he muttered, staring at the fountain.

"We've been friends for over a hundred years, Lathe," Sorbin reminded him solemnly. "Please tell me what's up. Did someone there upset you?"

"When it rains, it pours," Lathe murmured by way of answer. "That's all."

"What happened?" Sorbin insisted. "Whose ass do I need to kick?"

"No, no," Lathe hurried to answer. "Nothing like that. It's just . . . I—" Frowning, Lathe muttered, "You know I wasn't interested in finding my beloved. Not anymore."

Sorbin remained quiet for several heartbeats before murmuring, "Oh, Lathe. You met your beloved?"

"I think so. He's"—Lathe hesitated, rubbing over his thigh—"handsome and . . . perfect."

"I don't think anyone is perfect," Sorbin countered, although he sounded as if he sported a smile. "And why is that such a bad thing? Don't you think Fate knows what she's doing if she's giving you your beloved now?"

"You know I don't like to be touched," Lathe reminded his friend. "I don't even touch the occasional donor more than I have to, and gargoyles are a touchy-feely lot."

"You tolerate hugs from me and the guys," Sorbin pointed out. "And I can't imagine that you wouldn't enjoy the touch of your beloved."

Lathe hesitated an instant before blurting out, "He was about to fuck some gorgeous gargoyle when we walked into the room."

"Uhhhhh." Sorbin cleared his throat. "I'm not certain how to respond to that." Before Lathe could come up with something, Sorbin must have found his tongue, for he asked, "Did he stop whatever was happening with the other gargoyle?"

25

"Yeah, but I don't know if that was because Second Tobias and Enforcer Einan were with me or not."

"I would have stopped even if they weren't there."

Holden's deep soft voice rumbled from behind Lathe, startling him enough to drop his phone. He turned on the bench, gaping at the big male who stood just a few feet behind him. Between the fountain and the phone call, Lathe hadn't heard the gargoyle approach.

"And I hadn't planned to do anything with Tasker, anyway." Then Holden winced and added, "At least, not in your room." He rubbed the back of his neck, betraying his unease as he held Lathe's gaze. "I won't lie. I *have* fucked him, but that's all it ever was between us. A couple of guys scratching a mutual itch." Taking a step forward, Holden told him, "But now that I've met you, Lathe, that's all over with. You're my mate."

Lathe nibbled his bottom lip, uncertain how to respond to that.

When the silence stretched uncomfortably, Holden indicated the bench. "May I sit with you?"

Hearing Sorbin's shout through the phone snagged Lathe's attention, and as he picked up the device, he finally managed to get his mouth to work. "Um, sure."

Real witty, Lathe, he mentally berated himself.

# CHAPTER FOUR

Holden moved slowly around the bench, eyeing his clearly skittish mate. Having overheard most of Lathe's conversation with his friend—hearing he'd been called Sorbin—he knew just because Lathe was a vampire, it wouldn't all be smooth sailing. His mate didn't like to be touched.

*How can I change his mind on that?*

As a gargoyle, Holden had a high sex drive. He also enjoyed every aspect of love-making, from the kissing, touching, and petting of foreplay, to caring for his partner after the deed was done. He wondered how long, if ever, it would take for Lathe to allow him such liberties.

Lathe returned his phone to his ear as he watched Holden sit beside him. "Um, I'm sitting in the garden, and Holden just showed up," he told his friend. "He's sitting next to me."

"Let me talk to him," Sorbin demanded.

After a second of hesitation, Lathe held out his phone. "It's my friend, Sorbin," he told him. "He wants a word."

"Of course." Holden took the phone and placed it next to his own ear. "Hello, Sorbin. This is Holden."

"You're Lathe's beloved?" Sorbin stated bluntly.

"I am," Holden replied confidently. "He hasn't tasted my blood, yet, but I'm certain he's my mate."

"If you hurt him, I will flay your hide."

Holden couldn't help but smile upon hearing the threat even as he watched Lathe's eyes widen in surprise.

"Lathe is my mate," Holden repeated. "Should I accidently hurt him in some way, I would come to you for that flaying."

"He's had a hard life," Sorbin revealed. "You better be ready to make it better."

"That'll always be my goal," Holden confirmed, continuing to hold Lathe's gaze.

"Then you better be prepared to move to this clutch, Holden," Sorbin told him. "That'll make him happier." Before Holden could respond, he added, "And you better be prepared to protect him when Edward comes calling."

Growling softly, Holden asked, "Who's Edward, and why is he a danger to my mate?"

"I'll let Lathe tell you that story when he's ready," Sorbin replied. "Tell my buddy congratulations, and I hope to meet you soon."

Then Sorbin disconnected the line.

Holden held the phone out to Lathe. "He said congratulations." He smiled, pleased that his mate's friend was happy for them. As Lathe took the phone, he added, "Chieftain Maelgwn and the others offered their congratulations, too."

Lathe nodded once, then turned his attention to the fountain. His brows furrowed as he rubbed his palm over his left thigh. He remained quiet as he tucked the phone into an inner pocket of a light jacket he had on under the heavy coat.

Opening his mouth, Holden paused before saying anything. He closed his mouth, trying to decide how to get Lathe talking. He figured he might as well share that he'd overheard Lathe and his friend's conversation.

"Lathe, I heard you tell Sorbin that you don't like to be touched," Holden slowly began. "Does that include all touching? Or can I hold your hand?"

Holden took in Lathe's pensive expression, partially hidden by the length of black hair covering the left side of his face. His beautiful green eyes were narrowed, and he appeared lost in thought, hardly acknowledging Holden. He really wished he could tuck that hair behind Lathe's ear and draw the vampire's attention.

"Lathe?" Holden took a chance and reached toward Lathe. "Your hand?"

Ever-so-gently, Holden skimmed his fingertips along the back of Lathe's hand.

Lathe jolted, yanking his hand away and clamping it to his chest.

While that hurt, Holden did get what he wanted. His mate focused on him, peering at him with a wide-eyed gaze. The sharp movement caused the long hair on the left side of his face to wave, revealing scarring on his cheek for just an instant. Then Lathe stared at the ground while nibbling his bottom lip.

Holden scraped his left hand through his hair, struggling with what to say or do. Thinking quickly, he placed his hand palm up between them. Then he inhaled deeply before letting it out through pursed lips.

*Patience.*

"So, someone obviously told you my name is Holden," he began softly, focusing on the fountain in the center of the clearing. "I'm over four hundred years old, and I've been with this clutch for over half of that." As he spoke, he watched Lathe out of the corner of his eye. "I don't have a rank. I'm not dominant like that. I pull my weight by washing clothes and cleaning." Letting out a soft chuckle, he added, "And it's a good thing we have a great kitchen here because I can't cook for shit. I'm one of those guys that can burn water."

Finally, that seemed to get a reaction out of Lathe, for he let out a soft chuckle. "Me, either," he murmured. "I'm a tech guy."

"I saw you with a laptop bag," Holden commented, keeping his voice low and soothing. "Then you went to see Raymond, so that makes sense."

Lathe nodded before glancing his way, then down at Holden's hand. Ever-so-slowly, he lifted his left hand and moved it toward Holden's. He paused with their hands hovering close for a heartbeat, then two, before he rested his palm against Holden's own.

The touch, so light and innocent, still caused warm tingles to cascade up his arm. Butterflies jumped in his belly, and he swallowed hard. He sucked in a sharp breath before blowing that breath back out.

"Thank you," Holden whispered, curling his fingers around Lathe's in a loose hold.

"You probably think I'm a little, um, odd," Lathe murmured, once again staring at the fountain.

Holden shook his head. "Not at all, my mate," he countered. "Everyone has issues. We'll work through it." He would accept no less.

"Did you get into trouble with your chieftain?" Lathe asked, surprising Holden with his concern.

Shaking his head again, Holden replied, "No. Tasker did, but I didn't." Offering a smile Lathe's way, he added, "Thank you for your concern, though."

Lathe met his eyes for a few seconds, a small smile twitching at the corners of his lips. "Yeah." Then he licked his lips, and his attention slipped to Holden's pulse point.

Catching the action, Holden asked, "Do you want to taste me, Lathe?"

When Lathe blinked and returned his focus forward, Holden had to remind himself not to hold his breath as he waited for an answer.

"Th-That's okay," Lathe replied on a whisper. "I, uh, I had some bagged blood before coming."

Holden kept his mouth shut for a few seconds, barely holding back his desire to ask who'd donated to that bag. Hell, Lathe probably didn't even know. Still, his nature to provide for his mate spurred him on.

"We both know that's not why you'd want to taste me,"

Holden stated, squeezing Lathe's hand once more. "I'd love to provide for you. It would please us both." Unable to help himself, Holden smirked at his mate. "After all, I hear that donors come from the pleasure of a vampire's bite."

Lathe licked his lips. His chest rose and fell swiftly. Even his scent gave away his uncertainty.

"I-I suppose I could, um, take a bit from your wrist?"

While Holden would accept that if Lathe persisted, he decided to offer, "You can have my neck, Lathe." Tipping his head to the side, he touched his throat with his free hand. "I could kneel on the ground before you, making it easy for you to reach." Unable to help himself, Holden added, "Or if you'd prefer, you can straddle my thighs."

"You'd kneel for me?" Lathe sounded shocked.

"Of course," Holden responded easily. With a wink, he told his mate, "I'll be kneeling when I suck your dick, too, so why not for you to feed?"

Gaping, Lathe stared at him with wide eyes.

Holden held his gaze while reminding, "Lathe, I'm a gargoyle. I've been around for over four hundred years. I know how to please you." After a second, he added, "All I need is the chance."

For a couple of heartbeats, Lathe just stared back at him. Then his attention once again slipped to Holden's neck. He licked his lips before swallowing hard enough to cause his Adam's apple to bob.

"O-Okay," Lathe murmured huskily. "The neck is more intimate, and it'll scar."

"Good," Holden replied. "I want your mark as much as I want to mark you."

Lathe nodded once more.

When Lathe didn't make a move to climb onto his lap, Holden took the initiative. He eased from the bench. The cobblestones felt cold under his knees, but he ignored it in favor of sliding forward and sideways.

Continuing to hold Lathe's hand, Holden turned to face him. He gently rubbed the back of his soon-to-be lover's hand with his thumb. Hovering his right hand over Lathe's left knee, he saw the vampire tense, so he paused.

"Will you spread your legs for me, Lathe?" Holden asked, more than willing to use their paranormal natures to move their bond forward. "So I can get closer?"

Lathe did as Holden asked, spreading his legs wide. At the move, Holden felt his dick swiftly thicken. He couldn't help eyeing Lathe's fly as he eased between the man's legs. Desire to be between his vampire's legs for another reason rushed through him, and his cock began to throb.

*Be patient.*

With that mental reminder, Holden held Lathe's gaze. "Fair warning. I'm going to open my loincloth."

Lathe's nostrils flared as he dipped his attention down Holden's body. His green eyes began to bleed to red, and his chest sped up with each of his panting breaths. He parted his lips, revealing his fangs as he licked them, his anticipation apparent.

The scent of Lathe's lust filled Holden's nostrils, and he quickly did as he'd said, revealing his aching length.

"You're purple," Lathe muttered, his focus riveted on Holden's bobbing shaft. "All over."

"I am," Holden confirmed. "And my hair is green. Hope that's okay."

Lathe snapped his focus back to Holden's face. "You're stunning just the way you are." Lifting his free hand, he reached toward Holden's face. "So handsome."

Holden placed his left hand near Lathe's opposite hip, barely refraining from gripping it. With bated breath, he waited to see what Lathe would do. His patience was rewarded when Lathe teased his layered, shoulder-length hair away from his face, revealing his shoulder more fully.

"Lean forward," Lathe ordered as he did the same.

Obeying, Holden panted softly, his own anticipation ramping up. He felt his cock leak as Lathe rested his hand on his shoulder before leaning toward his opposite one. Holden tipped his head to the side, allowing him greater access.

"Gods," Lathe whispered roughly. "Y-You smell so good."

Before Holden could come up with a response, he felt Lathe lick up his neck. He moaned softly, his eyelids sliding to half-mast. His nipples beaded, and he groaned Lathe's name.

"Holden," Lathe muttered before licking him again. "So good."

Holden felt Lathe wrap his lips around the tendon of his neck. The prick of fangs caused his gut to clench. When Lathe scraped along his flesh, his balls began to tighten.

"Gods, Lathe," Holden mumbled, his voice deep with longing. "Y-You're going to make me come before you even bite me."

"Don't want that," Lathe muttered. Then . . . he bit, sinking his fangs deep into Holden's flesh.

The flash of pain only lasted an instant before a wash of ecstasy-inducing tingles erupted through Holden. He moaned his mate's name as Lathe's deep sucking pulls on his neck seemed to transfer straight to his cock. His prick jerked as his balls pulled impossibly tight.

Without a touch, Holden came, releasing his seed in blissful spurts. He dug his nails into the stone bench, fighting his need to clutch Lathe to him. Spots danced across his vision as he kept coming over and over.

Finally, Lathe eased his teeth from Holden's neck. He licked over the mark, sending a fresh shiver through him. When he began to draw away, Holden snapped open eyelids he hadn't even realized he'd closed.

"Wow," Holden murmured thickly, smiling upon seeing

Lathe's heavy-lidded gaze. "That was even more intense than I figured it'd be."

Lathe licked his lips and hummed. "You're delicious."

Holden could still scent Lathe's arousal, and a glance down told him how in need his mate truly was. The fly of his jeans was tented obscenely, clearly outlined by the fabric.

Lifting his left hand, Holden slowly moved it toward Lathe's fly. "You just gave me the most intense orgasm of my life," Holden admitted, holding his vampire's gaze. "Can I return the favor?"

For an instant, Holden worried Lathe would say no.

Then, to his relief and pleasure, his mate nodded.

Finally releasing Lathe's hand, Holden moved both to Lathe's fly. As he gently undid the button, Lathe leaned back a little to accommodate him. He unzipped, finding a pair of green boxer-briefs.

Holden gripped the waistband and eased them forward and down. When they were probably halfway down Lathe's shaft, his mate squeezed his neck, gaining his attention.

"That's far enough," Lathe whispered.

While Holden's first intention had been to tuck the underwear under Lathe's balls, he obeyed, releasing the fabric. He gripped the top couple of inches of Lathe's erection and tipped it up. Then he bent, opened his mouth, and wrapped his lips around the pre-cum dampened head.

Lathe's flavor exploded across his taste buds, heady and delicious. He suckled the crown, lapping at his vampire's slit. Slipping his thumb into his mouth, he massaged his frenulum, increasing the stimulation.

Gripping Holden's head, Lathe threaded his fingers through his hair.

Humming his pleasure upon feeling his mate's touch, Holden sucked strongly before scraping a canine across his flushed head.

Lathe called out Holden's name right before a burst of cum flowed across his tongue. He greedily swallowed it and sucked for more. His efforts were rewarded, Lathe coating his tongue over and over.

When Lathe stopped coming, Holden eased off his vampire's dick. He noticed the way the man's underwear had been pushed down a bit more from his ministrations. On the left side of his erection, close to the base, was puckered skin similar to his face.

Snapping his attention to Lathe's face, Holden whispered, "How extensive is the scarring?"

A second later, Holden landed on his ass as Lathe shoved him away, telling him that was definitely the wrong thing to say.

# CHAPTER FIVE

Tears burned the backs of Lathe's eyelids as he climbed to his feet. He grabbed his jeans. Before he'd even zipped and buttoned, he was already moving.

Lathe limped as swiftly away from Holden as he could. The whole reason he hadn't wanted the gargoyle to pull his underwear down further was so he wouldn't see his scars. The majority of his left side had burn scars, even the base of his dick and ball sack.

"Lathe, wait!" Holden cried, obviously following him. "Please."

Feeling Holden grip his arm, Lathe twisted his body and jerked his arm, tearing free. The sudden move sent a spike of pain through his weak leg, and he stumbled. Only grabbing a trellis saved him from a fall.

"Shit, shit, shit," Holden muttered, lifting his hands, palms out in placation, his loincloth dangling from his left one. He stood in front of Lathe, naked as the day he was born, peering down at him with pain in his bright amber eyes. "Please, Lathe. Please, stop and talk to me."

Lathe wrapped his arms around his torso, hugging himself. "Y-You weren't supposed to see."

"Oh, mate," Holden rumbled, easing a step closer. "I don't care that you have scars." He touched the left side of his own face, indicating that he'd noticed the ones on Lathe's face. "I only care in as much as to how they affect your health and wellness."

"I don't want you to see," Lathe muttered, turning and

walking again. "They're ugly. I'm ugly."

"You're not ugly, and neither are your scars," Holden declared, walking backward to keep up with him. "They're a badge of strength, heralding your survivalist spirit." As Holden spoke, he bent and wrapped his loincloth back around him. "They're just a part of who you are, and I wish you'd give me the chance to prove that I don't care about them." Once Holden had finished tying his stays, he reached out and rested his palms ever-so-lightly on Lathe's shoulders. "Please, mate. Don't run from me."

"Let me go," Lathe growled through gritted teeth.

Lathe wished he could give in to the urge to sink into Holden's embrace, but not being touched was too ingrained. It didn't matter that the weight of his beloved's hands felt fantastic. He would bet that getting a hug from the gargoyle would feel wonderful, too.

*And trilling. Gargoyles trill. Would he do that for me if I asked?*

Slowly, Holden lifted his hands, but he didn't move them far. "I'm your beloved, Lathe," he stated firmly. "And you're my mate." His voice grew thick. "It's killing me that I can't hold you when you're upset."

Taking a deep breath, Lathe met Holden's gaze. He saw the pain in the man's eyes and hated that he'd caused it. Fighting his trembling, Lathe eased a step closer.

"Will you trill for me?" Lathe whispered.

"Any time you want, Lathe," Holden crooned, opening his arms wider. "Always."

"Okay." With his arms still wrapped around himself, Lathe tucked against Holden's much larger frame.

With slow, gentle movements, Holden closed his arms around Lathe. He rubbed one palm up and down his back. He even closed his wings around them both, securing him in a cocoon of warmth.

Then . . . Holden started trilling.

The odd vocalization created a cascade of soothing vibra-
tions. They seemed to melt into Lathe, heating him from the
inside out. The sensations calmed his nerves, allowing him to
relax, truly relax, for the first time in . . . decades.

"Wow," Lathe mumbled, resting his cheek against
Holden's chest. "This feels amazing."

*Even better than Destrawn.*

Holden nuzzled his cheek against Lathe's head, then
pressed a kiss to his temple. His soft breaths warmed Lathe's
skin, causing his hair to stand on end. He pressed tighter into
Holden's embrace, realizing he never wanted the wonderful
sensations to end.

"I got you, Lathe," Holden rumbled, continuing to trill.
"We'll figure this out, you and I. I'm your beloved." He continued murmuring encouragement into Lathe's ear. "You
need my blood to survive. I know that." After another kiss,
this time to Lathe's ear, Holden whispered, "And you're my
mate. I've been waiting for you for so very long, and I feel so
truly blessed to have met you."

"I'm so messed up," Lathe mumbled, frowning at Holden's
deep purple skin. "Inside and out. I don't know how you can
think that." Taking a chance, he lifted his head and peered up
at Holden. "I haven't had sex since I was attacked."

"Being mates isn't all about sex, Lathe," Holden replied
quietly. "And I'd be more than happy for you to fuck me
first . . . when you're ready." He began to dip his head, then
paused, "May I kiss you, Lathe? Just a touch of lips."

Lathe couldn't remember the last time he'd kissed . . . anyone.

*Am I ready?*

*To please my beloved, I want to try.*

"Okay," Lathe whispered.

With wide eyes, Lathe watched Holden's head descend.
His amber eyes filled with heat. He continued to hold Lathe's
gaze, pausing with his lips a hairs' breadth from Lathe's. Then

he closed the distance, and Lathe felt the press of his beloved's mouth against his own.

Sighing, Lathe allowed his eyelids to slide closed. He pushed into the kiss, enjoying the firm feel. His body ignited all over again, arousal surging through him.

All too soon, Holden lifted his head, breaking the kiss.

Lathe would forever deny his whine of disappointment.

Holden smiled down at him. "Thank you, my mate." Trailing his hand up and down Lathe's spine once more, he stated, "My chieftain cleared my schedule for the next few days. Would you like to track down your chieftain and share the news with him?" After another few seconds of hesitation, he added, "Then we can curl up in my suite in front of the fire. Maybe have a glass of wine and a meal? Sunrise is in about three hours, and I'd like to spend that time with you."

Surprise filled Lathe. "It's that late, already?" Having been living with gargoyles for the past several months, he'd begun adjusting his schedule to accommodate them. Still, he'd never stayed up all night before.

"It is," Holden confirmed. "What do you say?"

Lathe nodded. "Yeah. I think I'd like that."

Even as he said the words, he was surprised at how true they were, too. He wanted to spend more time with Holden.

"Let's go then," Holden urged, easing his left wing and arm from Lathe. At the same time, he turned back toward the clearing with the fountain.

"Um, where?" Lathe began, starting to walk with his beloved.

Holden cleared his throat before telling him, "You, uh, you were actually heading deeper into the garden labyrinth."

"Oh." Lathe took in the high walls, trellises, and plants. "It's all starting to look the same to me."

"It can do that," Holden replied with a nod. "I could just fly us out, if you'd prefer."

"No," Lathe quickly answered. Seeing the way Holden's brow ridges shot up, he added, "Enforcer Sethnos carried me for hours this evening, and it really tightened up my thigh." Lathe figured it was an apt time to share. "A vampire named Edward kidnapped and tortured me, then left me for dead in a fire. I didn't get blood in time. So, to answer your earlier question" — if Holden was going to have a problem with his scarring, it would be better to know right away — "the scarring is all down my left side, but Edward cut up my left thigh, and my muscles will never be the same."

A low growl escaped Holden, but for some reason, the sound soothed Lathe as opposed to worrying him.

"Please tell me the asshole is dead."

Lathe sighed. "I wish I could. I thought he was, but —" With a grimace, he admitted, "He contacted me this afternoon. He's still alive, and now he's found me."

"Well, if he comes after you, I will very happily kill him," Holden snarled, curling his lip. "I'll keep you safe, my mate."

Pausing on the garden path, Lathe peered up at Holden. He took in his fiercely determined expression and the anger simmering in his amber eyes. Realizing Holden was upset on his behalf, Lathe smiled just a smidge.

"Thank you, Holden."

*Maybe Fate was right to send him a big strong protector.*

"Always, my mate." Holden took a deep breath, his ire draining out of his features as he blew it out. Then he smiled at him. "You're my life now. Bonded or not."

*Bonded. Right.*

"Um, about that, um, bonding." Lathe grimaced as he looked away. "I . . . I don't —"

"I told you," Holden cut in. He slid a hand up underneath his hair, cradling his left cheek. "Whenever you're ready."

Lathe froze, tensing in Holden's grip. He felt the gargoyle's hand on his cheek faintly through the scarring. His breath caught in his chest, and he stared at Holden, shock slithering through him.

Holden must have recognized his look, for his smile softened. "And I told you. I don't care about your scars." His fingertips teased along his jawline. "I care about them only insomuch as how they affect you. For example, can you feel my hand on you?"

"Yes," Lathe answered breathlessly. "A little."

After nodding, Holden dipped his head and pecked a kiss to his lips. "So, a bit more pressure to feel through them." He released Lathe's cheek and urged him to start walking again. "And you'll let me know if you're sensitive anywhere. I don't want to accidentally hurt you."

"Okay," Lathe found himself instantly agreeing.

"Good." As they walked, Holden commented, "We'll probably find your chieftain with his brother and mother." He hummed softly, before asking, "Will he mind the interruption?"

Lathe grimaced. He didn't like the idea of interrupting Chieftain Kinsey's time with his family, but he knew he needed to share what was going on, too. "It'll be fine, as long as we're quick," he decided. "He needs to know, after all."

"That was my thought, too," Holden admitted.

When they reached the house, Lathe told him, "This isn't my overcoat. Raymond gave it to me." He pulled away from Holden and began shrugging out of it. "I don't know where he got it."

"There's a coat closet over here," Holden told him, taking the article. "We keep a few spare overcoats as well as shoes and sweats." With a chuckle, he explained, "We never know when one of the shifters living here will need them."

"That makes sense," Lathe replied, watching him hang the coat in the closet he'd indicated. "I think there's something like that at our coven, uh, clutch." He shook his head ruefully. "Still getting used to that. There's a gargoyle mated with a lion shifter there."

Holden nodded. "Makes sense then." Returning to his side, he eased close and slowly wrapped his right arm around him, settling his hand on Lathe's hip. "This okay?"

"Yeah." Lathe smiled, surprised to find he was getting used to Holden's touches. "Thank you for checking."

"Always, my mate," Holden assured. "The infirmary is on the first floor beyond the cafeteria. This way."

Lathe didn't bother responding, just following Holden's cues. They eventually came to a set of double swinging doors.

Holden pushed one open, and they entered a small waiting room. There was a large, pale green gargoyle sitting behind the desk. He was reading on an electronic device, but he looked up when they entered. The gargoyle swept his gaze over them in an assessing manner.

"Hi, Holden," the male greeted. His gaze focused on Lathe. "Your friend is limping. You need me to help with something?"

Grimacing, Lathe shook his head. "It's a permanent old injury."

"Hi, Doctor Perseus. This is Lathe. My mate." Holden sounded so damn proud of that. "Is Chieftain Kinsey still here visiting Wendy?"

"Yes," Perseus answered, rising to his feet. "And congratulations. I assume you want to see him?"

"Yes, please," Holden confirmed.

Perseus rounded the desk and headed toward a closed door. Pausing at it, he knocked lightly. Upon hearing a male voice order him to enter, the doc did so.

"Hey, doc," a man greeted. "We getting kicked out?"

"Not yet," Doctor Perseus countered. "Lathe and Holden are here to see Chieftain Kinsey."

"I'll be right out," Chieftain Kinsey replied. "Right after I share one more bit of important news with my mom."

"What is it, dear?" a female answered, a definite note of fatigue in her voice. "Is everything okay with your clutch?"

Lathe figured that was Wendy.

"Everything is fine, Mom," Chieftain Kinsey replied, confirming Lathe's supposition. "I just . . . I'm hoping what I'm about to share will help perk you up . . . at least for a while."

"Oh, honey." Wendy sighed. "Sometimes, it's just time, sweetheart."

"I know." Chieftain Kinsey definitely sounded sad. "But I was hoping you'd fight long enough to see your first grandson."

"G-Grandson?" Wendy whispered. Then an excited cry filled the air. "Oh, honey. Are you telling me what I think you're telling me? Are you pregnant, Jimmy?"

"Yes, ma'am," Jimmy replied, sounding pleased as punch. "I'm pregnant. Three weeks now."

"Oh, wow. Congratulations!" Wendy's voice sounded stronger already. "You bet your cinnamon that I'll find a way to stick around. Now come here, Jimmy, and tell me all about how you're feeling. Kinsey, go see what your people need."

"Yes, Momma." Amusement laced Chieftain Kinsey's voice. A few seconds later, he appeared from the room. "Hey, Lathe." He arched one yellowish-orange brow as he glanced between them, obviously taking in the way Holden held Lathe. "Lathe? Something you wish to share?"

Lathe nodded once. "Yes, Chieftain Kinsey." He waved his hand to indicate Holden. "This is Holden. He's my beloved."

"Really?" As Lathe nodded again, Chieftain Kinsey's features took on a concerned tilt. "And are you going to be okay with that?"

When Lathe had joined Chieftain Kinsey's clutch, he'd had to explain everything—his past and hang-ups—with the chieftain.

After nibbling his bottom lip for a few seconds, Lathe quietly admitted, "I haven't told Holden everything. We were going to get a meal and sit down together." He cast a side-eyed look his beloved's way, seeing the concern filling his eyes. Then he refocused on his chieftain. "But he's my beloved, and I'm his mate. I need to figure out how to make this work."

Chieftain Kinsey nodded once, his expression softening. "Congratulations, Lathe." Then he grimaced. "Am I going to be losing you to this clutch?"

"No, sir," Holden answered for them. "I already know that Lathe would be happier staying where he's at." Dipping his head in obvious submission, he added, "I'll be putting in a petition to join your clutch soon."

"Good," Chieftain Kinsey replied. "It'll be granted."

# CHAPTER SIX

Holden managed to keep his questions to himself until they reached his suite. As he placed the tray of food they'd picked up from the dining hall on his coffee table, he glanced over his shoulder at Lathe. His mate stood several feet away, holding the bottle of wine and glasses, looking distinctly uncomfortable.

"Please, come and make yourself at home." Holden stood and grabbed a blanket off the back of his sofa. After spreading it on the floor between the coffee table and the fireplace, he grabbed a couple of throw pillows and tossed them onto the blanket. "Are you okay to sit on the floor?" It suddenly occurred to him that with Lathe's scarring, it could be uncomfortable for him. "We can sit on the sofa instead."

"The floor is fine," Lathe murmured, moving closer.

As Lathe put down the wine and glasses, Holden turned to his fireplace. He quickly started a fire, watching Lathe out of the corner of his eye. His mate opened the screw-cap off the wine, then poured them both a glass.

Once Holden had the fire well in hand, he moved to Lathe's side, settling on one of the pillows on the blanket. He bent his knees and crossed his legs before him, getting comfortable. Then he held up his hand, palm up, offering to help Lathe lower himself to the floor beside him.

Lathe glanced from his hand to the floor, then reached out and took it.

Pleasure radiated through Holden when his mate settled beside him. After releasing him, he began setting up the food.

He'd grabbed a platter of assorted cold items—finger sandwiches in turkey, tuna, and roast beef. There were deviled eggs as well as *Jello* salad. He'd also grabbed prosciutto wrapped in cheese, and he even remembered cold cinnamon rolls for dessert.

"So, you alluded to the fact that you still had more to your story to tell me," Holden finally broached. "Is that something you want to do now or later?"

Lathe gripped the base of his stemware and slowly rotated the glass. He stared pensively at the liquid for a moment, not responding as Holden filled a small plate with items and placed it in front of him. He was halfway making up his own plate when Lathe let out a long sigh.

"Well, it has to do with our completing our bond," Lathe began softly before lifting his glass and taking a sip of wine. "I know you said you'd give me all the time I need, but what if I'm never ready?" Lathe focused on Holden and told him, "I haven't had sex since being attacked. Giving or receiving. For the most part, I couldn't even get hard."

Holden smirked. "You mean, the blowjob I gave you broke one hell of a dry streak for you?"

Lathe's eyes widened for an instant before he snorted. "Yeah," he muttered. "Guess you did." Then he rubbed his palm over his left thigh . . . a move Holden was quickly coming to recognize Lathe did when he was uncomfortable.

"You can tell me anything, Lathe," Holden encouraged. "We're mates, and we need to be able to communicate."

"Edward told me over and over that he was going to fuck me, but he wanted to break me first," Lathe revealed roughly. His expression turned a little vacant as he continued, "He wanted me to answer to Pet and to call him Master. I refused, so he beat me. Then he grew his claws and cut me. He refused to allow me blood to heal." Clearing his throat, Lathe told him, "I would have rather died than give in to him, and if it

weren't for Sorbin going against our coven master and tracking me down, I would have."

"Sorbin had to go against your coven master in order to
rescue you?" A fresh wave of rage rose up within Holden.
"What the fuck?"

Then Lathe explained about their ultra-conservative coven
in Alabama.

"Anyway, the master claimed this was Fate punishing me
for being gay," Lathe muttered dryly. "We still don't know
how the fire started, but Sorbin dragged me out of it. He hid
me in a hotel room, fed me his blood at first, then bagged
blood once I'd started to heal." Meeting Holden's gaze, Lathe
explained, "Thinking about sex, all those things he did to me
fill my head. It sorta kills the mood."

Holden nodded slowly, thinking he understood. "So,
you're worried that if you tried to fuck me, you wouldn't stay
hard, even though I'm your beloved?"

Lathe swallowed so hard his Adam's apple bobbed.
"Yeah." After a few seconds of hesitation, he added, "And I'm
afraid that if you get near me with your dick, I'll freak out."

Unable to help himself, Holden pointed out, "But the blowjob seemed just fine."

"A blowjob isn't sex."

Picking up his own glass of wine, Holden took a sip.
"Okay. Well, like I told you before." He smiled, trying to re-
assure his mate. "Finishing the bond can be done with fingers,
tails, and bites. Full-on sex never has to happen between us."

Clearly confused, Lathe asked, "What do you mean?"

Holden nudged Lathe's plate closer to him, then picked up
a roast beef sandwich from his own plate. "Well." He popped
the food into his mouth and chewed the tasty morsel. To his
pleasure, Lathe followed his lead, picking up a stuffed mush-
room. Once Holden had swallowed, he stated, "One of the

gargoyles here bonded with his mate by jacking into a condom, then inserting the collected cum into his mate's ass."

Lathe coughed around his mouthful of food, clearly surprised. After taking a sip of his wine, he gaped. "Really?"

Holden nodded. "And Enforcer Einan doesn't bottom, so he must have sucked off Cornelius a million times to finish their bond and go through molt."

"How do you know this about your clutch-mates?" Lathe asked, staring in surprise. "Do you guys just sit around talking about sex?"

Chuckling, Holden shook his head. "Naw. But on long winter nights where those of us who don't have a human form are stuck inside due to the weather, we don't have a lot to do but gossip." Smiling ruefully, he told his mate, "There aren't too many secrets in a gargoyle clutch. Only if the couple agrees ahead of time never to mention it to anyone else." With a wink, Holden said, "Like the marriage vault. Only discussed between the married couple."

"Huh." Lathe obviously didn't know what to say to that, so he ate a turkey sandwich.

"Anyway, what I'm saying is, there are workarounds that we can use," Holden assured. "Then, when or if you ever feel ready, we'll explore more together." Reaching over, he squeezed Lathe's wrist lightly for a few seconds. "I'm just happy to be able to hold you, Lathe. Please believe me when I tell you that."

Lathe nodded, a tentative smile curving his lips. "I believe you."

"Thank you." Holden returned to eating, letting his mate relax and process that.

Once Holden noticed that Lathe was slowing down, only taking a bite every few minutes, he pushed his own plate away. Then he crawled over to the fire and added a couple more logs. Once he had the blaze roaring, he stretched out on the blanket, crossing his legs at the ankle.

"Join me?" Holden spread his right arm wide, hoping Lathe would take him up on the invitation.

To Holden's pleasure, after only a second of hesitation, Lathe did. His vampire sprawled next to him before easing closer. He settled beside him, curling toward him on his left side.

Then Holden saw the wince.

Realizing what he'd done, he grimaced. "Shit, Lathe. I'm sorry." He eased to a sitting position. "Let's switch sides. You'll be more comfortable. Right?"

Lathe nodded. "I really will."

"Not a problem." In seconds, Holden was up and over Lathe. He lay back down to his vampire's right. "Let's try this again."

Warmth filled Holden's gut when Lathe immediately cuddled up beside him, curling into his side. With a sigh, Holden curved his left arm around him, teasing his fingertips up under the hem of his shirt. He felt the scarring there and petted it absently.

Tensing, Lathe frowned at him.

"I told you," Holden reminded him. "It doesn't bother me. If this hurts, I'll stop, but otherwise, I'd really like to touch you."

Blowing out a harsh breath, Lathe relaxed a little. "It'll take some getting used to, but I'll try."

"That's all I can ask for." Turning his head, Holden pressed a kiss to Lathe's temple. "So, other than computers, what do you like to do for fun?"

Lathe hummed. "Guess I don't have a lot of hobbies or anything," he told him. "Sorbin and I have two buddies still at the vampire coven. Donny and Vicon. They visit a lot."

For the next hour, Holden asked questions about Lathe's

friends. They talked about Holden's duties at the clutch, and Holden shared a few silly tales that happened to friends.

When Holden felt the pull of sunrise, he banked the fire. Then he walked his mate to his own suite to rest. As he flew to the roof and settled down to roost, Holden prayed to any gods who cared to listen that soon he wouldn't have to be forced apart from his mate by the sun.

*Besides, how can I protect him from Edward if I can't be with him during the day?*

# CHAPTER SEVEN

L athe slept sounder than he would have thought possible while visiting a strange place. He didn't know if it was the result of the brain-melting orgasm, the couple glasses of wine he'd drank with Holden, or the relaxing cuddling they'd done. Maybe it was a result of all three.

All Lathe knew upon waking was that he'd managed a full nine hours of sleep, and he hadn't had a nightmare.

Swinging his legs over the side of the bed, Lathe rubbed his hands over his face. He glanced at the clock, surprised to see it was after four in the afternoon. Rising to his feet, he stretched his arms over his head and twisted one way, then the other.

His thigh twinged a little, but that wasn't anything new.

After rolling his head on his neck from shoulder to shoulder a couple of times, Lathe's bladder made itself known. He headed to the bathroom and used the facilities. Lathe turned on the shower before stripping, folding his sleep pants and shirt, and placing them on the counter to be used the following night.

Easing into the spacious shower, Lathe stood under the water for several minutes, just enjoying the sensation. Then he washed up. When Lathe scrubbed his hands over his dick, he began to plump.

Lathe's lips twitched in amusement. It seemed, after one blowjob from his beloved, his libido was returning. Peering intently at the scarring over the left side of his body for the first time in years, Lathe truly wondered what Holden would think of his form.

The ridges of puckered flesh continued down the left side of his ribcage and across his hip. It extended to his groin, just touching the base of his dick and the side of his ball sack. In truth, he'd been lucky not to lose his testicles. The obvious differences in his thighs were the hardest thing to look at.

Edward had used his claws to carve out a hunk of his muscle, telling him, "If it hurts to stand, you'll get used to being on your knees."

Dismissing those memories, Lathe refocused on thoughts of Holden. The gargoyle had been so sweet, kind, and understanding. He'd been patient and gentle, and Lathe quickly realized he'd only pushed when he thought it was in Lathe's best interests—like hugging.

Lathe smiled as he turned off the water.

*I really like being held by Holden.*

Wanting more of that, Lathe looked forward to nightfall. He grabbed a towel and dried himself off. Wrapping it around his waist, he moved to the sink, finishing off his morning routine by brushing his teeth and blowing dry his hair, making the thick wave on the left fall across his cheek.

After dressing in comfortable jeans and a polo shirt, Lathe pulled on socks and sneakers, humming in anticipation of finding some food. When he'd been greeted by Second Tobias, he'd been assured that the dining hall was open twenty-four-seven. That hadn't always been the case, but with nearly all their gargoyles mated, their chefs could take turns with the day and night shifts, giving everyone access to fresh food all the time.

Ready to face the day, Lathe paused at his laptop. Unable to resist, he opened it and fired it up. He was curious if Ninevah had been able to find anything.

Upon opening his emails, his good humor and hope fled. He had another message from his stalker.

*Your friends won't be able to find me, pet. No one can. Don't worry. I'll visit you soon, so we can pick up where we left off.*

Gulping, Lathe wrapped his arms around his torso. He rocked a little in his chair, unable to tear his gaze off the words.

*Pick up where we left off.*

Lathe would rather die.

Except, where would that leave Holden? He needed to think of the well-being of his beloved. If they did manage to bond, then Edward killed him—that would mean the end of Holden's life as well. As much as Lathe loved the feel of his arms around him, he couldn't put his gargoyle at risk.

"So, that means I need to get rid of the bastard," Lathe whispered, trying to pull himself together. "But how?"

Lathe already knew he was no match in a fight with the other vampire. Even when he'd been healthy, Edward had been stronger and faster. He'd easily subdued him and taken him from the club.

Reading the message again, Lathe frowned. Somehow, Edward knew that he had friends looking for him.

*How?*

Pulling out his phone, Lathe dialed Ninevah's number.

"Hi, Lathe," Ninevah greeted after the second ring. "Sorry, I don't have anything for you, yet."

"I have something for you," Lathe stated without preamble. "He's contacted me again, and he knows that I have people looking into him."

Ninevah remained quiet for a couple of seconds. Then he grunted before ordering, "Forward the new message to me. I have a hunch."

"What?" Lathe asked even as he did as the other vampire bid.

"If I'm right, he's embedded a worm in his emails," Ninevah told him. "That way, he'll be alerted to where they go." He snorted. "Got the message. He's a bit creepy, isn't he? Okay, I'm going to check into this. I'll get back to you soon."

"Thanks, Ninevah." While Lathe was good with technology, he wasn't much of a hacker. Plus, he was having a difficult time keeping his head where Edward was concerned. "I appreciate it."

"Sure, Lathe." Ninevah already sounded distracted. "Oh, now might be a good time to get the Vampire Council involved. They should know that whoever reported Edward dead wasn't doing their job."

"Right." Lathe frowned. "How do I do that?"

"If Chieftain Kinsey doesn't have a contact, call Master Krispin. He'll help you."

"Of course." Lathe winced. "Brain's not working well, I guess."

"Not surprising, all things considered," Ninevah replied. "Later." Then the fellow vampire hung up.

Blowing out a deep breath, Lathe decided it was time for a cup of coffee. Plus, he would need to track down his chieftain. He knew what room Chieftain Kinsey and Jimmy were assigned, so he made his way there, first. Not surprisingly, when he knocked, he didn't get an answer.

Lathe headed to the cafeteria next. After a quick sweep of the room, he spotted another one of the clutch's tech guys—Vane. Raymond had mentioned him a few times the prior day, and his description was spot on.

Vane sported a blood-red hide, red eyes, and black wings and horns. His face seemed flatter than most gargoyles. His eye sockets were hollower, and his nose appeared a bit sunken, causing his brow ridges to appear more pronounced and giving his face an almost skull-like visage.

As Lathe crossed to the counter and poured himself a cup of coffee, he wondered if he had the courage to approach the male. He added creamer to his coffee, then glanced over his shoulder. Spotting a slender, brown-haired man sit down next to Vane and get a kiss from the massive gargoyle, Lathe decided to risk it.

Quickly, Lathe grabbed a plate and placed two pre-wrapped sausage, egg, and cheese breakfast burritos onto it. He followed that up with a scoop of fried potatoes and a small cup of picante sauce. Lathe tucked a napkin-wrapped roll of silverware under his arm, picked up both his plate and coffee, then made his way toward the pair.

Lathe hesitated a few seconds, noticing that they sat alone. Girding up his courage, he finished making his way over there. He found himself pinned by Vane's red-eyed gaze as he took the last half-dozen steps.

"C-Can I join you?" Lathe appreciated that his voice didn't squeak.

The brown-haired guy — a human, from his scent — smiled up at him. "Sure, man." He waved at the bench seat across from them. "Have a seat." Once Lathe had sat down, he reached across the table. "I'm Matthew. Call me Matt."

Taking the man's hand, Lathe shook. "I'm Lathe." He'd heard from Raymond that Matt was Vane's mate. "Nice to meet you."

Matt nudged Vane's shoulder. "This is my mate. Vane."

Lathe didn't try to take the male's hand. Instead, he dipped his head in acknowledgment. "Uh, Vane."

Vane grunted before rumbling, "Lathe."

"So, uh." Lathe began unwrapping one of the burritos. "I, uh. Well, Raymond told me you were a hacker."

Vane stabbed his fork into a bite of rare steak as he dipped his chin in a nod. After popping the dripping meat into his mouth, he arched one eyebrow ridge in silent question.

Lifting his cup of picante sauce, Lathe poured it onto the end of his burrito. "Did Raymond share my problem?" Then he took a big bite of his food and couldn't resist humming appreciatively.

"Your stalker," Vane replied on a snarl. "Yeah. He showed

me the programs he's using to search for him. They look good."

Lathe nodded, chewing and swallowing. "I received another message from Edward this morning." Just saying the other vampire's name caused his hunger to wane, but he refused to give in to it. Instead, Lathe poured more sauce on his burrito, and before taking a big bite, he added, "Edward knows I have people looking for him. He says no one can find him, but he'll visit me soon . . . to finish what he started."

Vane's smile appeared a little creepy. "That's good. Then we can kill him."

Sucking in a surprised breath, Lathe began choking on his food. He coughed, trying to gasp around the food. Lifting his napkin to his mouth, he did his best not to spray his half-chewed burrito across the table.

Lathe felt a hand gently patting his upper back, and he glanced over to see Bobby, Chieftain Maelgwn's mate. The human glanced between the group, worry etched on his features. His green eyes held a wealth of concern.

Once Lathe could breathe, he took a sip of his coffee. That helped, so he took a deeper one. Finally feeling in control, he wiped his mouth and straightened.

Bobby sat down next to Lathe on the bench seat, placing a cup of coffee before him. "Wow." He arched one black brow. "What was that all about? You okay, Lathe?"

While Lathe figured he shouldn't have been surprised that Bobby knew who he was, he found he was after all. "You know me?" he gasped.

Waggling his brows, Bobby grinned. "Of course. You're Lathe, Holden's mate," he answered brightly. "Congrats, by the way." Then Bobby cocked his head and focused on Vane. "What'd you say to shock the shit out of him?"

Vane smirked. "I told him we'd be happy if Edward came around. That way, I could kill him."

Bobby rolled his eyes, obviously not at all surprised by Vane's blood-thirsty nature. "Well, I think we should get permission from the Vampire Council before we kill off some random vamp."

"He's a rogue," Lathe claimed. He forced himself to return to his food, using his fork to stab a fried potato chunk. "They thought they'd killed him decades ago, but I guess not."

"Huh." Bobby wrapped his hands around his mug. "Then we should let them know they were wrong."

While Vane just grunted, clearly unimpressed, Matt nodded.

Lathe quickly swallowed so he could say, "That's what Ninevah recommended." Seeing the question in Bobby's green eyes, he explained, "That's my ex-coven's tech guru. He's searching for Edward's whereabouts, same as Raymond." As Bobby continued to nod, Lathe quickly added, "Thank you for your help, by the way."

Bobby smiled as he pulled out his phone. "You're welcome." Then he started scrolling through contacts on his phone. "I don't have a number for the Vampire Council, but I do have the next best thing." With a grin, Bobby claimed, "My ex is bonded with a vampire master near Santa Fe. I'll give him a call."

Matt snickered. "Maelgwn's okay with you calling your ex?"

"Eh, we didn't end on terrible terms," Bobby claimed, hitting the call button. "Plus, Maelgwn and Adalric have worked together a number of times."

Lathe assumed he was referring to the vampire master.

"Bobby?" A man's deep voice came through the line — Lathe's acute vampire hearing allowing him to hear both sides of the conversation — and the guy sounded more than a little confused.

*Evidently, they don't talk much.*

"Hi, Seth," Bobby greeted, sounding happy. "How are you

and Adalric doing?"

"We're good, good," Seth replied, his tone easing. "Uh, how's life with a kid?"

Lathe had heard that not too long before, Bobby had blessed Maelgwn with an egg. He hadn't yet asked about the tyke, but he figured he would have to be around two years old now. Lathe wondered if the little one wasn't with Bobby because of their guests. He knew gargoyles were damn protective of their young, since they were so rare.

"Fantastic. Donahue is on a play date with Cornelius and Einan's son. Did you know Cornelius is pregnant again," Bobby replied with a laugh. "But anyway, that's not why I'm calling."

"I figured not," Seth replied. "What's up, Bobby?"

"I need a contact for the Vampire Council," Bobby stated without preamble. "They need to know that one of their enforcers pronounced a rogue dead, but he's really not dead." A low growl entered his tone. "And the asshole is threatening a friend. I want deets."

Seth groaned. "Damn. That sucks. Hang on."

Bobby winked at Lathe as silence came over the line.

Then Seth returned, saying, "I have Adalric here with me. Tell us the details."

Staring pointedly at Lathe, Bobby arched one brow.

Discomfort flooded Lathe as he glanced around the cafeteria. Fortunately, every other occupied table was on the other side of the room. He figured that was due to Vane's reclusive nature.

"This is Lathe Mantuvian," Lathe began. "Thank you for speaking with me, Master Adalric."

"Of course, Lathe," Adalric replied. "I assume you are the one being threatened?"

"Yes, Master," Lathe replied. Then he took the next five minutes to share an abridged version of what had happened to him almost fifty years before.

When Lathe finished speaking, Adalric growled softly. "This rogue has been loose for over fifty years," he snarled. "Yes, we definitely need to figure out who botched the job. Give me just a moment." Through the line, although his voice was faint, Lathe heard Adalric say, "Lex, how soon can you get to my office?"

Lathe didn't hear Lex's response, but Adalric responded with, "Good. See you in five."

Then Adalric seemed to refocus on their call, for his voice grew louder. "Lexington Paistro is an ex-Council Enforcer. He'll have better contacts than having to go through official channels." He chuckled roughly before saying, "And we'll get a much faster and more discreet response."

Lathe was all for fast and discreet. He desperately wanted this all to end.

# CHAPTER EIGHT

For several seconds after waking from roost, Holden sat crouched on the roof. He was filled with a wash of anticipation, and it took him a few seconds to place it. Then he grinned, jumped to his feet, and hurried to the edge of the roof.

*My mate.*

Holden spread his wings and jumped. Swooping to the left, he found his balcony ledge on the second floor. He landed and headed inside.

As much as Holden wanted to get straight to tracking down his vampire, he needed to clean up first. That didn't mean he wasn't going to do it as swiftly as possible. After peeing and brushing his teeth, Holden took the fastest shower possible.

Normally, Holden enjoyed standing under the spray and reveling in the heat of a hot shower. The invention of indoor plumbing had been one of the most wonderful, in his opinion. No longer did he have to scrub in a cold river or spend hours heating water over a fire.

Instead of drying his hair, Holden pulled it back from his face. He used a piece of leather to tie it at his nape, giving him a small tail. Then he hurried from his suite.

Holden headed through the halls to the guest wing. He found the door where he'd left Lathe the evening before, and a fissure of nerves trickled up his spine. After taking a deep breath to steady himself, Holden knocked.

Cocking his head, Holden listened closely. He didn't hear

any movement beyond the door. After a moment, he knocked a second time.

Still receiving no response, Holden inhaled deeply. His mate's scent was reasonably fresh, but he could tell Lathe hadn't been there recently. He'd probably left his suite a good half an hour before.

*Could my mate be avoiding me?*

Holden rubbed the back of his neck, wondering if something could have happened during the day that might have driven his mate away. Holden had thought he'd made great strides in securing Lathe's affections the prior day, as much as a few hours could anyway, but his vampire was wary and shy. Something could have renewed his reservations.

With concern churning in his gut, Holden strode through the estate. He headed for the dining hall. He hoped someone there would be able to point him in Lathe's direction. Plus, it would give him a chance to grab something to eat and drink.

*If I don't see him there, I'll check in Raymond's security office.*

With his plan in mind, Holden trotted down the main hall stairs. He hurried to the doors and pulled one open. Stepping inside, he swept his gaze over the room.

The relief he felt upon seeing Lathe sitting at a table off to the side, his laptop open before him, caused his shoulders to physically sag.

*My mate.*

Striding that way, Holden didn't quite reach him before another gargoyle beat him there.

Tasker settled on the bench across from Lathe, and Holden picked up his pace.

"Hi, Lathe," Tasker greeted, drawing his vampire's attention. Holden knew he wasn't the only one who noticed the stiffening of Lathe's shoulders when Tasker lifted his hands, palms out, in obvious placation. "I came to apologize."

Lathe's eyes narrowed. "Apologize for what?"

Holden had to give Lathe props. His vampire wasn't going

to make it easy for Tasker. He was making the other gargoyle spell it out.

Tasker ran his blue hand through his white hair as he scoffed. "Hell, where to start, right?" Then he began ticking things off on his fingers. "Trying to fuck in your room is probably the top of the list. I shouldn't have tried seducing Holden in there, either. He'd already said he wasn't interested, but I was trying to change his mind. Also wrong." Resting both palms on the table, Tasker's voice turned rueful. "I know you didn't know you were mates at the time, but that doesn't make any of those things okay. And now"—he waved one hand as he shook his head—"gods, I'm jealous as hell."

Stopping to Tasker's left, Holden smiled at Lathe. To his pleasure, Lathe smiled back at him.

Peering over his shoulder at him, Tasker muttered, "Hey."

"Hey," Holden replied, a little uncomfortable to be in the presence of his mate as well as an ex-fuck-buddy.

*Guess it's a good thing I'm going to be moving to Lathe's clutch.*

"I don't blame you for being jealous of me," Lathe murmured, a small smile curving the corners of his lips. "I mean, who wouldn't want to be mated with Holden. He's a catch."

Holden grinned broadly upon hearing his vampire's praise.

*Okay. So my mate wasn't trying to avoid me.*

Tasker scoffed rudely as he shook his head. "Naw, I'm not jealous of you, Lathe." With a shrug of one shoulder, he cast a dismissive glance at Holden before giving Lathe an appreciative once-over. "I'm jealous of Holden. I mean, how could I not be?" Waving his hand up and down, Tasker indicated Lathe. "You're lean and hot. You're a vampire, which means you could easily top me. You're perfect."

Lathe gaped at Tasker.

While Holden silently agreed with everything Tasker had just said, he couldn't help the low, jealous growl that escaped him. After all, they weren't bonded yet.

Turning to straddle the bench so he could face them both, Tasker rolled his eyes. "Aww, come on, man. You know I'm right."

"Of course, I know you're right," Holden replied through gritted teeth. "Lathe *is* perfect. That doesn't mean I like seeing and hearing that you're checking him out."

"I-It's kind of flattering," Lathe mumbled, drawing Holden's attention. He had one arm wrapped around his torso in a half-hug while he touched the left side of his face under his hair. Issuing a partial shrug, Lathe muttered, "Cause I'm anything but perfect."

"Oh, my mate." Holden hurried to Lathe's side and dropped onto the bench beside him. After a second of hesitation, he wrapped his arm and wing around his mate, tucking him close to his side. "You know I don't care about the scars."

Lathe cuddled into his side, warming Holden from the inside out. "I know you don't."

Tasker chuckled as he shook his head. "You two are so cute." Then he grinned and rose to his feet. "And Holden's right. Those scars mean one thing. You're a survivor." With a wide grin, Tasker urged, "Wear them with pride, man."

Then Tasker headed toward the breakfast bar.

"Huh." Lathe's brows furrowed. "That was . . . something."

"Tasker really is a good guy," Holden told him. "He's just . . . friendly."

"Well, I hope he finds his mate soon," Lathe commented dryly. "That way, he'll be a little more circumspect on who he's *friendly* with."

Holden chuckled. "Yeah." Then his stomach growled. "You mind if I grab some food?"

Lathe shook his head. "Not at all. That's why I'm working on my laptop in here." With a smile, he told him, "I figured you would turn up eventually."

Humming, Holden couldn't resist, so he dipped his head and pecked Lathe's lips. "I tried your room first," he admitted. With a chuckle, he added, "Must have been how Tasker beat me here." After giving Lathe's gorgeous lips one more butterfly kiss, Holden rose and touched his vampire's shoulder. "Be right back."

Then Holden hurried to fill a plate. As he loaded his tray with several pre-made sausage, egg, and cheese sandwiches on English muffins, Tasker sidled up beside him. "Hey, you and Lathe doing okay?" he muttered, giving him the side-eye. "I didn't botch things up too bad for you, did I?"

"You didn't do anything. Not really," Holden assured, giving his friend a smile. "Every couple has some hurdles to get over."

"You're talking about his scars," Tasker stated astutely. "I scented how he seems to feel about them." Before Holden could decide what he was willing to share in regards to his mate's past, Tasker continued, "And he limped out of the bedroom yesterday. He must have been through something damn traumatic for a vampire to be scarred. Fire?"

Holden nodded once. "Among other things."

"Damn," Tasker muttered, frowning. "Well, if you need help with anything, let me know, eh?"

Even though Holden couldn't imagine asking Tasker for aid, he still nodded. "I appreciate the sentiment."

Tasker nodded, accepting that. Then he headed to a table where a few others were sitting.

Holden scooped a large dollop of scalloped potatoes onto his plate to go with his sandwiches. Then he headed toward the drink station. He made himself a cup of coffee. Turning, Holden spotted the mug beside Lathe's laptop, and he couldn't remember how full it was.

Taking a chance, Holden filled a second mug and placed it

on his tray. He didn't know how his vampire took the beverage, so he grabbed a couple of creamer cups as well as several sugar packets. As Holden headed back to the table, he vowed to notice how Lathe prepared it.

Placing the tray on the table, Holden moved the extra cup of coffee off the tray and beside Lathe's nearly empty mug. "I wasn't certain how you liked it," he admitted as he sat. "So I brought these." Holden offered the creamer and sugar.

"Thank you." Lathe graced him with a shy smile. "I appreciate it."

Holden watched carefully as Lathe opened the creamer and added it to his mug. Then he swirled the mug and took a sip. He hummed and nodded.

"That's good," Lathe murmured after swallowing. "I sometimes forget I have a drink, and it gets cold." Making a face, he stated, "Nothing worse than cold coffee. Yuck."

Chuckling, Holden nodded, making a note to always have a refresher coffee ready in case Lathe wanted it. "What are you working on?" he asked curiously as he unwrapped his sandwich. Waiting on the answer, he took a big bite and hummed appreciatively as he chewed.

"This is the security schematics of the Aerasceatle clutch's estate," Lathe told him, turning the laptop a little to show him. "After reviewing your security here, I realized we had a few gaps. I'm isolating them and figuring out how many more cameras we need."

"You handle security single-handedly?" Holden asked, impressed. "Wow."

Lathe chuckled as he shook his head. "Naw, not single-handedly. The entire inner circle has a say." He pointed at circles and notations on the screen. "This is just a proposal. Once I get home, we'll all review it and go from there."

"That's still impressive," Holden claimed before taking another bite.

"So, what are you supposed to be doing today?" Lathe asked curiously, turning his laptop back to face him.

Holden shrugged. "I have the next couple of days off." He knew he'd told Lathe that the prior day, but between the stress of the meeting and their initial getting to know each other, he figured his vampire hadn't remembered. "So, I guess I'll hang out with you. We can talk. Get to know each other some more. Pack my suite." Waggling his eyebrow ridges, Holden lowered his voice to a husky rumble as hope for just how well they would be able to *get to know each other* filled him, and he added, "Unless you'll find my presence too distracting."

Lathe's nostrils flared. A flush rose up his cheeks, turning them a lovely shade of pink. The sweet scent of Lathe's arousal teased Holden's nostrils, and he groaned softly.

"Lathe," Holden moaned softly. "Gods, Lathe. I—"

"Hey, Holden. Lathe. Sorry to interrupt."

Chieftain Maelgwn's deep voice pulled Holden out of his lustful thoughts. Even as he acknowledged that was probably a good thing—after all, Lathe was shy, and they were in the dining hall—he wanted to groan in frustration. He stifled it, however.

"Hello, Chieftain Maelgwn," Holden greeted, returning to focusing on his food. "I'm always honored to have you join us."

The corners of the chieftain's dark-blue lips twitched, but he didn't call Holden out on his . . . stretch of the truth. He settled across from Holden. To Holden's surprise, they were also joined by Bobby, as well as Chieftain Kinsey, Enforcer Sethnos, and Second Tobias—each man cradled their own drink. From their scents, they varied from coffee, wine, beer, and soda.

"Bobby told me about the phone call he made to Seth and Adalric," Maelgwn stated without preamble. "I've had a call back from Adalric, and he says Lexington got in touch with Enforcer Vince Marché. He's just up in Stone Ridge, so he and his wolf shifter mate are going to zip down here for your statement." Frowning, Maelgwn added, "He has access to closed files, so he should be able to figure out what the hell happened back then."

"Really?" Lathe's brows shot up. "That fast?"

"Wait. What's going on?" Holden wasn't following the conversation. While he knew who Seth and Adalric were, he wasn't certain of the others. Focusing on Lathe, worry crept up his spine. "Did something happen?"

"You didn't tell him, yet?" Chieftain Kinsey sounded surprised as he glanced between them.

"I just woke from roost," Holden explained, defending his mate. "We were just catching up while I ate breakfast."

"Roost?" Chieftain Kinsey hummed as he nodded. "Ah. Still working on completing the bond."

"I told Lathe I'd give him as much time as he needed," Holden added, reaching over to place his hand on Lathe's thigh. "We'll get it done when he's ready and I'm ready."

Chieftain Kinsey nodded. "Fair enough."

"So, what do we need to do to prepare for this vampire enforcer's arrival?" Holden asked before he again added, "And, uh, what's going on?"

Lathe rested his hand on top of Holden's, giving it a squeeze. His smile appeared tight, but he shared everything that had happened earlier in the day—from finding a second message from Edward to his talk with Ninevah to discussing it with Bobby, Vane, and Matt.

Holden winced when he heard Vane's calloused comment, but he couldn't help but think the other gargoyle had the right idea. If he had the chance, he wasn't certain he would bother taking the vampire alive. The man was after his mate, after all. Killing him would technically be well within his right.

"Anyway," Chieftain Maelgwn continued. "I think Gus used to play poker with Frankie. I'm going to go ask him about them."

"Uh, Frankie?"

Holden was glad that it was Lathe who asked.

"Vince's wolf shifter mate. It's why they were in Stone Ridge," Chieftain Maelgwn explained. "Frankie's brother still lives there, so they have a house in residence and are both considered members." Rising to his feet, Maelgwn glanced between them both. "Anyway, congratulations again, and we will figure this out. Enjoy your day, and I'll contact you when they arrive." After a second of hesitation, Maelgwn warned, "It'll probably be during the day, though."

With those words, Chieftain Maelgwn left, followed by Bobby and Second Tobias.

Chieftain Kinsey leaned forward, resting his forearms on the table while wrapping them around his beer. "I don't mean to push, but do you think you're going to be able to complete your bond this evening, Lathe?"

Lifting a hand, Holden murmured, "Please, Chieftain. I gave my mate my word. We'll get there, but—"

"I ask only because I know your need to see to Lathe's safety is probably driving you nuts," Kinsey cut in, holding up a hand in placation. "I'm not going to sugarcoat this. If Edward has been able to stay off the council's radar for this long, he's a dangerous vampire. We all must be vigilant." Kinsey pointed at Lathe. "That means you need to have your gargoyle by your side."

Lathe tightened his hold on Holden's hand. "I know, Chieftain." His voice came out barely a whisper. "You're right, but the answer is . . . I don't know."

While Holden appreciated the honest answer, even if he didn't like it, he mentally ticked off names of mated gargoyles that he could go to for help.

# CHAPTER NINE

Lathe followed Holden into his suite and set his laptop bag on a cushioned chair in the living room. Nerves skittered through him, but he wasn't certain how to banish them. His hands felt empty without the bag strap to cling to.

Sighing, Lathe rested his good hip against the chair's arm and crossed his arms over his chest.

When Holden finished starting a fire, he turned and straightened. He crossed to him, holding his hands out. When he was close enough, Lathe slid his palms into Holden's, which earned him a grateful smile.

"I know why Chieftain Kinsey was encouraging you to allow us to finish our bond," Holden began slowly, obviously choosing his words carefully. "But please, know that I stand by my word. We'll wait until you're ready." Before Lathe could answer, Holden quickly added, "I do understand the danger, and it's true that I'd prefer to be standing by your side through it all . . . but" —he smiled confidently at Lathe—"I have plenty of mated friends here. If I ask, they will be more than happy to keep you company during the day when I cannot."

"It isn't that I don't want to bond," Lathe replied, wondering how to convey his concerns. "I just . . ."

"Just what, my mate?"

Lathe lifted Holden's hand and brought it to his lips, kissing the back of one lightly. "I just don't want you to be disappointed when you see me." Grimacing, he whispered, "I'm really, really not perfect. I don't even like looking at myself,

69

so I can't imagine how you could possibly tolerate it. I—"

Holden growled softly as he lifted his fingertips to Lathe's mouth, ceasing his rambling.

"In this, I hope you'll allow me to assuage your fears, Lathe." Holden heaved softly as he frowned at the floor for a moment. Then he focused on Lathe again and asked, "I'm a gargoyle." He took a step backward and spread his arms wide. "Even for a gargoyle, my coloring is a little odd. Some would call me ugly. A monster. But you don't, do you?"

Scoffing, Lathe shook his head. "Of course I don't see you as a monster." Grimacing, he quickly added, "But having dark purple skin, green hair, and amber eyes is a bit different than having scars over about a quarter of your body." Lathe waved toward Holden even as he admired all the leathery skin on clear display. "You're stunning."

"And like many paranormals, we're attracted to someone by their scent," Holden pointed out. "I don't care about scars. I care about your scent and what's in here." He touched Lathe's chest lightly. "When your scent is pleasing, I'm happy. If you're upset, I'm upset, and I want to do whatever I can to change it so you smell happy again." Scoffing, Holden shrugged. "Do I want to smell your arousal and cover you in my own scent? Hell, yeah, but that's a normal desire for any paranormal couple." Narrowing his eyes, he eased a step closer while dipping his head. He rumbled in Lathe's ear and asked, "Can you honestly say you don't want to cover me in your scent?"

Lathe groaned softly as he nodded. "Yes," he admitted. "I want you to smell like me so badly."

"Well, there's a sure-fire way to do that," Holden pointed out. "We get naked and rub all over each other. Our sweat, our seed, our pheromones. I want to carry it all."

Sucking in a harsh gasp, Lathe lifted his chin and peered up at Holden. He read the sincerity in the gargoyle's eyes. His beloved wanted him in the most primal of ways.

"I want that, too," Lathe admitted. "I . . . I . . ."

"You're afraid," Holden whispered, revealing he did truly understand. "You're afraid the second I see you naked, I'll be turned-off."

Lathe nodded. "Yeah."

"It won't happen," Holden stated, his voice full of confidence. "But the only way for you to know that for certain is for you to allow me to see you." Turning away, Holden crossed to the sofa. Once again, he spread the blanket before the fire. Then he added a couple of pillows. "How about we start simple."

Then Holden whipped off his loincloth and tossed it aside, revealing his swollen erection. The purple length stretched from his groin, long and thick. The foreskin was partially retracted, and a bead of pre-cum was pooling at the tip.

Lathe's mouth watered, and he swallowed hard. His fingers twitched with his desire to touch, and he licked his lips with his yearning to taste. Clenching his hands into fists, he took a tentative step forward.

"H-How is that simple?" Lathe had to ask.

Holden grinned, showing off plenty of sharp white teeth. "Well." He pointed at his blatant arousal. "This way, you'll have more than just my scent to go by." Smirking, Holden stated, "If I'm turned-off by something, you'll know." His eyes narrowed, and his voice grew husky. "Same as if you'll know if I'm turned on by something, too." Lifting his arms out to his sides, Holden offered, "No secrets."

Slowly, Lathe nodded, understanding what Holden was getting at. If Lathe's body did turn Holden off, his body would betray him.

Easing onto the blanket, Holden rested on his butt while wrapping his tail around his right leg. He held up his left hand. "You don't have to get undressed, but I'd still like you to join me. Whatever happens will be up to you."

As Lathe slowly approached his brazen gargoyle, he knew he had to make a choice. He could either stay hidden away by his wall of clothing, or he could take a leap of faith. Holden would accept him either way.

Except, Lathe knew if he didn't at least try, then he would never know.

*Am I brave enough?*

A line from one of his favorite movies popped into his head. Spoken by a timid scientist when asked to walk into a nest of aliens to retrieve a communications device, the man mumbled to himself, "Acquiring courage . . . acquiring courage."

Lathe mentally chanted that to himself as he pushed away from the chair. Pausing beside the sofa, he eased down on it. He saw Holden's flinch as he lowered his hand and mentally berated himself for giving his beloved the wrong idea.

"Just taking my shoes and socks off," Lathe explained.

Holden nodded, watching with obvious interest as Lathe put deed to word.

After toeing off his sneakers, Lathe bent and removed his socks, tucking them into his shoes. Then he pushed back to his feet and crossed to the blanket. He paused at the side and scrunched his toes in the plush carpet for a few seconds.

Once more picking up his mental chant, Lathe gripped the hem of his polo shirt. He paused an instant and took a deep breath before pulling it over his head. Fighting his immediate instinct to cover himself, Lathe instead focused on folding his polo shirt and setting it over the arm of the sofa.

Then Lathe peered down at Holden. The gargoyle was smiling up at him. His cock remained hard, and his pleasure bled through in his scent. As soon as Lathe met Holden's gaze, his gargoyle lifted his hand once more.

Lathe took it and allowed Holden to help him onto the blanket. When Holden began gathering him close and tucking him against him, Lathe relaxed and went with it. He found himself cuddled against Holden's massive body, and his right side was pressed to his expansive torso as they lounged back on the pillows.

Holden rested his left hand on Lathe's side, palming the bumpy skin there. Placing his right hand on Lathe's belly, he started tracing over his abdominals. He traveled up a little, then back down, before starting back up again. Sometimes, Holden teased along the edge of his scarred skin before moving on to his other side.

At first, Lathe lay tense in his arms. He just couldn't seem to help himself. He couldn't ever remember being touched in such a manner. Even before Lathe's injuries, due to his location and coven, he'd never had a lover. He'd had fuck-buddies.

What Holden was doing to him felt . . . reverent. His gargoyle seemed to be mapping his skin, caressing each inch of his flesh. He dipped his head and nuzzled Lathe's temple, occasionally licking at the sweat that the fire caused.

Slowly, Lathe found himself relaxing until he sagged in his strong arms, content to just lie there, regardless of how much his cock throbbed behind the fly of his jeans. He lowered his eyelids to half-mast and just basked. The petting felt so wonderful, easing all of his nerves.

Lathe found his attention snagged by Holden's erection. His long purple dick lay hard and leaking against the gargoyle's abdominals. He had his right knee bent, his leg propped up, putting his heavy balls on clear display.

The gargoyle was obviously aroused, but he seemed content just to touch, enjoying their quiet time together.

Finally, Holden murmured, "I need to stoke the fire, my mate." He pecked a kiss to Lathe's temple before whispering, "Please don't go anywhere."

Then Holden eased away from him. He rolled to his knees,

his enormous black wings billowing above him. His arm muscles bulged pleasantly as he opened the metal fence, then placed a couple of logs into the fireplace.

Unable to help himself in his relaxed state, Lathe reached up and traced his fingertips over one leathery appendage. He thought it felt buttery soft and strong. The wing shifted and twitched under his touch.

It took a few heartbeats for Lathe to notice that Holden had stopped moving. He'd sat back on his calves and had bowed his head. His hands hung at his sides, and his fingers twitched.

"Holden?" Lathe whispered, wondering what was up. He stroked over Holden's wing again, hoping to draw his attention. "Are you okay?"

When Holden spoke, his voice was deeper and gruffer than Lathe had ever heard it, sounding full of strain. "N-Never had a-anyone pet my wings b-before," Holden rumbled. "W-Was always taught not to allow another to do that."

Yanking his hand away, Lathe muttered, "Oh, shit. I-I'm sorry." Then he recalled having been warned never to touch the wings or tail of any of the gargoyles living in Master Krispin's coven. He'd never asked why it was taboo. He'd just obeyed. "Oh, gods, Holden." He rocked forward onto his ass and wrapped his arms around his upturned knees. "I'm so sorry. I didn't mean to . . . mean to . . ."

Lathe didn't know what he'd meant to do other than, well, touch the enticing appendage.

"You misunderstand me, Lathe." Holden finally turned and looked at him. His eyes blazed with fierce arousal. "I loved every second of it. Wings and tails" — he heaved a deep breath before finishing—"they're an erogenous zone. Intimate. Reserved for our mate." Turning further, Holden eased onto his ass. "I didn't move because my control was slipping."

Gasping, Lathe stared at Holden's genitals. If at all possible, the purple had darkened. His foreskin had withdrawn fully, revealing his damp head and leaking slit. Even Holden's balls appeared to have swollen.

"Oh, gods," Lathe whispered, taking in Holden's heaving chest and his hungry expression. "I-I did that to you?"

Holden nodded once. "Yes, my mate." He glanced down at himself, shifted in obvious discomfort, then refocused on Lathe. "And I'm really going to have to do something about it or . . ." His voice trailed off on a grimace. "I'm a little . . . uncomfortable."

Lathe nodded, understanding blue balls even if he hadn't experienced it in decades. Of course, seeing Holden like that, scenting the heavy undertones of his arousal, he was quickly getting there himself. The pressure of his fly registered, and he suddenly wanted to see where this could go more than he wanted anything in his life.

"I-I want—" Lathe paused with his hands at his fly.

With his attention riveted to his groin, Holden murmured huskily, "Anything, Lathe. Anything you want."

"F-Frotting?"

Holden groaned as he reached down and gripped the base of his prick. "Gods, yes," he stated on a groan. "I want to smell like you so very badly."

Lathe wasted no more time. He unbuttoned his fly, lifted his hips, and pushed down. When Holden grabbed the hem of his jeans, he didn't fight it when his gargoyle tugged the fabric from his body. Once Holden had tossed aside the jeans, Lathe eased onto his back and sprawled nude before another for the first time since . . . Sorbin had tended his burned body.

Pushing that thought from his mind, Lathe focused on Holden. He watched the gargoyle's expression darken, heat turning his amber eyes nearly to liquid gold. A low growl rumbled from him as he eased onto his hands and knees.

Ever-so-slowly, Holden prowled toward him. His gaze roved over Lathe, and the hunger in his expression only seemed to intensify. Placing his hands on either side of Lathe's hips, he lowered his head.

Lathe gasped when, instead of opening his mouth and sucking his dick, Holden nuzzled his cheek against his length. Groaning, he slid his chin over his leaking crown, essentially marking him with his fluids. Then he pressed a decadent, suckling kiss to his glans before lifting up, swiping his tongue over him in the process.

Groaning, Lathe could do little but lie there and pant. His cock throbbed in the best of ways, and his gut clenched with the good kind of butterflies. He waited with anticipation for Holden's next move.

Holden didn't disappoint. He continued up Lathe's body, spreading his legs to straddle him. Bracing over Lathe, Holden slowly lowered his body, resting some of his weight upon him, providing delicious pressure on his cock.

Groaning, Lathe couldn't help but buck his hips. He grabbed for Holden's shoulders, needing something to ground him. His gargoyle hummed and grinned at him, his look one of feral delight.

Then Holden reached between him and gripped his erection in a loose hold. He moaned upon feeling the decadent stroke of his gargoyle's calloused palm. His breath rushed from him as he watched Holden press his cock against his own . . . then slip his foreskin over both their heads.

Lathe moaned Holden's name as he lowered his groin, applying pressure to their docked pricks.

"Gods, I love the sound of you calling my name," Holden growled, sliding his hand up Lathe's torso, stopping to tweak his nipple. "So sexy. So gorgeous. So mine."

Holden dipped his head as he began to rut his hips slowly, and Lathe couldn't stay still. He moved in counterpoint, planting his feet so he could push up against him. His cock ached, and his balls threatened to pull tight.

"Don't fight it, Lathe," Holden rumbled. "Look at me."

Blinking open eyelids he couldn't remember closing, Lathe stared up at Holden. His gargoyle fixed him with a gaze so full of lust and need, wonder and affection. He grinned, showing off his sharp teeth.

"There you are, my mate," Holden crooned, rutting harder. "Gonna mark you now. Gonna bite you. Ready?"

Lathe sucked in a sharp breath as anticipation spiked through him anew. "Yessss," he hissed, wanting that even more than his orgasm. Tilting his head to the side, offering his neck, Lathe urged, "Claim me."

"I will," Holden assured gruffly. Then he lowered his head and nipped lightly on the flesh where his neck met his shoulder, sending a jolt of pleasure through him. "Just as soon as you come."

As if to facilitate that, Holden pushed one last time, tilting his hips just right. The move caused pressure on Lathe's balls, jolting fiery tendrils of bliss through his system. Groaning Holden's name, Lathe didn't fight it when his testicles pulled tight, and his orgasm slammed through him.

Seconds later, the sharp pain of teeth piercing his flesh stabbed through him. Then . . . ecstasy.

# CHAPTER TEN

Holden eased his teeth from Lathe's neck before licking his tongue over his vampire's flesh. Gently, he lapped up every last trace of his man's delicious, life-giving fluid. His saliva also had the added benefit of sealing his bite mark.

As Holden stared at Lathe's neck, he hummed with smug satisfaction. He'd given his mate a blatant claiming scar. Any time Lathe wore anything that didn't require a tie, it would be on clear display.

*Gorgeous.*

"You're looking like the cat that ate the canary."

Chuckling huskily, Holden pulled his attention away from his bite mark and met Lathe's heavy-lidded gaze. "Mmmm, that look on you is just as good as the bite mark I left on your neck." He waggled his eyebrows playfully.

To Holden's pleasure, Lathe chuckled softly. "I like seeing my mark on you, too." As he spoke, he lifted his fingers and traced their pads over the claiming scar he'd left the evening before.

His mate's touch sent a zing of awareness through Holden. He groaned as his blood heated anew. A shiver went down his spine as tingles spread through him.

"Wow," Holden muttered as he eased to Lathe's right side. Grinning at Lathe, he told him, "That's an amazing sensation."

Lathe grinned up at him. "Glad to hear it."

Holden swept his gaze over Lathe, loving the relaxed lines of his body. His mate finally seemed naked and comfortable with him. He found his attention snagging on all the spilled semen coating Lathe's belly.

Holden swiped the tips of his forefingers through the mess. He knew some of it was his own, while even more was his mate's. He'd gotten his sexy vampire off twice, since he'd claimed him, after all.

Lifting it to his mouth, Holden wrapped his lips around his digits. He'd tasted himself plenty of times over the years, and he recalled the slightly salty flavor of his vampire. Smiling, he hummed as he swallowed the tasty treat.

Unable to help himself, Holden found his gaze sliding down Lathe's body to his groin. His vampire's legs were slightly splayed, his semi-hard cock and balls on lovely display. He licked his lips, wondering . . . wondering . . .

"What's going through that mind of yours, Holden?" Lathe asked softly.

Yanking his attention back to Lathe's face, Holden saw his vampire's look of concern. He licked his lips once, twice, then decided to voice his request. After all, all his mate could say was no, that he wasn't ready.

Holden slid his forefinger through their seed once more and held up his finger. "May I put this in you?"

Lathe's brows shot up. He opened his mouth, then closed it again. Finally, he nodded and parted his lips once more.

Realizing Lathe had gotten the wrong impression, Holden shook his head just a little. He also eased his hand toward his vampire's groin. Tipping his chin, he indicated down his vampire's body.

"Oh," Lathe breathed. He took in a deep breath, his chest expanding. Then he let it out just as slowly. After another couple of heartbeats, he nodded. "Okay."

Holden continued to wait, letting Lathe set the pace. To his pleasure — and relief — his vampire spread his legs. His heart thundering in his chest with anticipation, he teased his middle finger along Lathe's balls and beyond. Holden glanced between Lathe's face, the strong lines of his body, and his groin. When his mate remained relaxed and complacent beneath him, Holden found Lathe's hole and teased his middle finger over it.

"Go ahead," Lathe murmured, moving his left leg and spreading them wider. "Bond us."

Groaning with excitement, Holden did as he'd been bidden. He pushed his finger into Lathe's body. To his surprise, Lathe moaned softly and rocked his hips, pushing against him.

"Oh, wow," Lathe whispered on a groan. "So good. More." He fixed his gaze on Holden. "More seed. We want to make certain it takes."

Holden froze for a few seconds, then nodded quickly. He eased his finger out and scooped up another dollop. After slipping that into Lathe, he wriggled it around, searching.

Lathe groaned and arched, pleasure etching across his features. "So good. Again."

Obeying, Holden watched transfixed as he pushed dollop after dollop of their combined seed into Lathe's chute. His mate groaned and panted, rocked and sighed, clearly enjoying every second of it. His vampire's erection once again jutted from his body, and Holden found himself in the same state.

As much as Holden wished he could replace his fingers with his dick, he knew Lathe wasn't ready to go that far. Besides, that wasn't what was needed to finish their bond.

"Lathe," Holden rumbled while scratching his fingers along the shaved right side of his vampire's skull. "Need you."

Humming, Lathe opened his eyes and stared at him with a heavy-lidded gaze. "What do you need?" He practically slurred the question.

"C-Can I . . . ride you?" Holden's chute clenched, and he knew he needed lube, but he needed permission first.

Lathe swept his gaze over Holden's massive frame, his eyes opening a little wider. "Y-You want to?"

"More than anything," Holden confirmed.

Glancing at his own groin, Lathe seemed to take in his heavily aroused state. Then he refocused on Holden. "Gods, yes, my beloved. I want to feel you so bad."

Moaning with excitement, Holden leaped to his feet. "Gotta get lube," he cried, sprinting from the room. His cock smacked his abs every few steps, spurring him on. He grabbed it from his nightstand, then hurried back to the living room.

To Holden's pleasure, Lathe hadn't moved an inch. He still lay before the fire, sprawled and aroused. His sweaty skin gleamed in the firelight, and the debauched smile he wore was truly the most beautiful thing Holden had ever seen.

After dropping to his knees beside Lathe, Holden popped the cap on the lube. "Do you know what one of the best things about being a gargoyle is?" he asked as he poured a healthy dollop of the viscous liquid onto the last couple of inches of his tail.

"What's that?" Lathe asked. He had his brows furrowed, and he stared in obvious interest.

Chuckling, Holden closed the lube before tossing it aside. "I have a tail." He straddled Lathe once more and winked at him. "A third appendage."

Then Holden dipped his head, cradling Lathe's jaw with his clean hand. As he sealed his mouth over his vampire's lips, he pressed his tail into his own ass. He groaned into his mate's mouth, enjoying not only Lathe's amazing flavor, but also the sensation of opening his ass.

Holden lapped his tongue over Lathe's, then sunk deeper.

Mapping and tasting, teasing, and touching, he learned his vampire, encouraging him to tease and taste in return. Before long, they dueled, and Holden backed off, allowing Lathe to take the lead.

When breathing became paramount—and Holden's cock throbbed from his ass-play—Holden broke the kiss. He panted harshly, trying to catch his breath even as he levered up and pulled his tail from himself. As Holden knee-walked backward a little, searching out the perfect position, he admired the hungry gleam in his vampire's red-irised eyes.

*Oh yeah.*

Not able to wait an instant longer, Holden reached behind himself. He gripped Lathe's cock and guided it to his hole.

"Ready?" Holden paused, needing his mate's acceptance one last time.

Growling, Lathe showed off his fangs. "Do it now," he ordered. "Fuck yourself on my cock."

Holden groaned, realizing he must be seeing a spark of Lathe's original personality . . . and he loved it. He did as he was told. Pressing back, feeling Lathe's cock head touch his ring, Holden pushed out and took his vampire's erection in deep.

Groaning loudly, Holden arched his back as he settled on Lathe's groin. He shuddered with pleasure, feeling his vampire's erection press against his gland. After a few panting breaths, Holden heard the unmistakable sound of tearing fabric. He managed to open his eyes and peer down at Lathe.

Taking in the stunning visage of his aroused beyond reason vampire, Holden gave his mate a feral grin. "Love it when I drive you so wild your eyes turn red," he declared.

Then, regaining some control, Holden arched his back and placed his hands behind his head. Spreading his wings, Holden flapped gently. He used the momentum to lift and lower himself at the perfect angle, pegging his gland over and over again. Tipping his head back, Holden groaned deeply, reveling in the exquisite sensations cascading through him, made all the better by the knowledge that this was his mate.

"Oh, fuck, Holden!"

Lathe's cries of delight caused Holden's own arousal to burn hotter. His balls ached, and his cock throbbed. His chute rippled along the length he rode, and his gut clenched. Even his nipples beaded, and he knew his orgasm approached.

Needing Lathe to come with him, Holden sped up his wingbeats, bounding faster and harder on his vampire's dick.

Suddenly, Holden felt Lathe's clawed hands dig into his hips, and he knew his mate was there. Taking him deep one last time, he stilled with his lover's erection spearing him. Giving up the fight, Holden groaned as he welcomed his orgasm, his balls unloading and painting his vampire's torso with streak after streak of seed.

Holden hummed with bliss, reveling in the feel of Lathe's hot cum coating his rectum and how his lover's erection twitched and pulsed within him. Peeling open his eyelids, he stared down at Lathe as lethargy began to sweep over him. He grinned upon seeing how his mate's irises had bled to red once more. Seeing the hunger there, Holden knew what his mate wanted.

Lowering his arms, Holden eased forward. He tipped his head to the side.

Lathe immediately took the offer. He lunged upward and sank his fangs deep into Holden's neck. The spark of pain disappeared with one swipe of tongue around his fangs, replacing it with the most exquisite tingles. Bliss surged through Holden's veins, and he groaned as a third orgasm within the course of an hour crashed over his senses.

Whispering Lathe's name, Holden shuddered and jerked within his vampire's hold. He felt his eyes roll as black spots danced across his vision.

Succumbing to the sensation, he blacked out.

When Holden woke, he still lay sprawled before the fire, which roared steadily, telling him Lathe must have tended to it. Turning his head, he shifted on the blanket. His chute muscles twinged in a way that felt good and odd all at the same time.

It'd been a hell of a long time since he'd bottomed, but for his mate, he was more than happy to.

Turning his head, Holden searched for said mate. When he didn't see him right away, he frowned. Then, over the crackle of the fire, he heard his vampire's soft, limping footfalls.

Holden focused on the bathroom door and smiled when he watched it open. There, in a halo of bathroom light, stood his gorgeous vampire. Holden noticed his mate held a couple of cloths, one in each hand.

"Hi, babe," Holden rumbled huskily. "Sorry I passed out." Stretching his body, he smiled at his mate. "But damn, did all that feel amazing."

Lathe returned his smile as he moved toward him. "Good." His expression turned a bit pensive. "Because I heard molt is hella-painful for you all if you don't have your mate there to soothe you."

"Yup," Holden confirmed. "Heard that, too." As he watched Lathe lower to the floor, he cocked his head a little. "You gonna be here with me, Lathe?"

With a wide-eyed look, Lathe gaped at him for a second. Then he snapped his mouth shut and frowned at Holden. "Of course, I'm going to be here with you." Then his eyes narrowed as he began wiping the warm, wet cloth over Holden's stomach. "Don't tell me you're one of those big strong morons who think they have to go it alone."

Holden chuckled as he shook his head, tickled pink that his mate was willing to clean him. "I'd love to have you here, my mate." Touching Lathe's wrist, he added, "I heard it can be a little grotesque, is all. I don't want to gross you out."

Lathe rolled his eyes, then indicated his left side, which was still bare to Holden's gaze—much to his pleasure. "Hello. I know what grotesque really is." Furrowing his brows, he grumbled, "You should have seen this shit when it was healing." Curling his lip, Lathe muttered, "That was grotesque."

"Then we're in agreement," Holden stated, not bothering to address the grotesqueness of Lathe's healing. After all, many wounds looked absolutely revolting while working through the stages of healing. "In the morning, when my life sucks for a few minutes, you'll be there to help soothe me."

"Damn straight," Lathe muttered. "Spread your legs."

Biting back a chuckle, Holden did as he'd been ordered, spreading his legs and accepting Lathe's ministrations. After all, how could he not love that his vampire wanted to care for him?

Hours later, when Holden went through the pain-wracking process of molt, he couldn't imagine how a gargoyle could withstand it without his mate by his side.

It was damn near agony.

# CHAPTER ELEVEN

"No," Holden gasped, shaking his head, his sweat-soaked brown hair waving around his face. "No shower yet. Help me up."

Confused as hell, Lathe still did his best to do as his mate urged. He wrapped his arm around Holden's human-looking shoulders. As he helped his gargoyle in human form rise to his feet, he had to admit, he missed the purple and green.

*Not that I'll ever tell Holden that, because he's handsome in this form, too.*

Lathe figured he would have to beat off the competition with a stick anytime he went out with Holden. The man's six-foot-four, broad-shouldered and slender-waist frame was just too enticing — to both males and females. His eyes had darkened to a golden chocolate color, and his square-jawed features had softened to an aristocratic, chiseled look.

*In a word — stunning.*

When Lathe took a step on his left leg while supporting Holden, he almost went down. Only his gargoyle grabbing the doorknob to the French doors caught them both. He managed to get his weight on his right leg as Holden turned the knob.

"What are we doing?" Lathe asked, confused as hell.

What could be so damn important outside that Holden needed to get out there first thing after molt?

"Sunrise," Holden muttered, his voice still thick with fatigue from going through molt. "Wanna see it."

Lathe frowned for an instant even as they carefully maneuvered out the door. "The sunrise?" Then it hit him why something like that would be so important to a gargoyle. Holden lived in perpetual darkness. "Right. Okay."

Keeping his mouth shut, Lathe gritted his teeth, doing his best not to groan with the pain of helping Holden to a deck chair positioned on the balcony. As soon as his gargoyle in human skin was seated, he squeaked in surprise. Holden grabbed his waist and urged him onto his lap.

Knowing better than to fight his beloved's strength, Lathe went with it. He ended up on Holden's thighs, with his lover's arms clasped tightly around his waist. His beloved nuzzled his face into Lathe's neck as he relaxed on the chair.

"Never seen a sunrise," Holden whispered into his ear. "Always wanted to share my first one with my mate." Sighing, he rubbed over Lathe's arms. "Shoulda remembered a coat. This form is a little cold."

Lathe smiled and turned his head. He saw Holden's disgruntled look and almost chuckled. Instead, he offered, "Want me to go get that blanket off the living room floor?"

Holden hesitated, then nodded. "If it's not too much trouble."

Shaking his head, Lathe murmured, "Not at all." Finding a streak of playfulness upon sensing his beloved's weakness from going through molt, he teased, "Of course, you're going to have to release me to do that."

Snorting, Holden nodded. "Very well." Then his grip eased.

Taking advantage, Lathe quickly rose and limped swiftly into Holden's suite. He not only grabbed the blanket, but he snagged his shoes and socks as well.

Once Lathe returned to the deck, he put down his shoes before spreading the blanket over Holden. Then he pulled his socks from his shoes before pushing his feet into the sneakers.

Finally, he moved to Holden's feet and slipped his own socks onto his beloved's feet. They were probably a little tight, but considering they were outside in the chilly morning weather, they were better than nothing.

"Thank you, my mate," Holden murmured, smiling at him. He held out his arms. "Please come here."

Lathe did as Holden bid, and he slipped under the blanket where his gargoyle held it up. While it wasn't quite as comfortable when his lover was a slightly smaller size, he still curled up in his arms, relaxing against his chest. Tucking close, Lathe kissed the base of Holden's throat, then turned his attention to the sunrise, enjoying the hues of gold and pink.

Groaning softly, Lathe tried to stretch. He felt the arms around him tighten and smiled. Easing his eyelids open, he hummed as he took in Holden's relaxed, sleepy expression.

At some point, Lathe realized they both must have dozed. He decided being held by Holden was so much better than the last time he'd been held by someone. As much as he appreciated Sorbin, Lathe didn't like waking with his friend holding him due to nightmares.

"What are you thinking about?" Holden asked curiously, arching one brow.

Deciding to be honest, Lathe admitted, "That this is so much better than the last time I woke up in someone's arms."

Growling softly, Holden scowled at him. "Was that Edward?"

Lathe scoffed and shook his head. "Uh, no." Wrinkling his nose, he told him, "He would never lower himself to the level of caring for someone." He dismissed his thoughts of his time with that asshole and admitted, "Actually, I was thinking of waking in Sorbin's arms a time or two after a nightmare." Knowing he needed to be honest, Lathe admitted, "I do still have them on occasion. Nightmares."

Holden nodded slowly. "I'm sorry that happened to you." Then he nuzzled Lathe's temple before nipping behind his ear. "And I'm glad you enjoy this so much more."

Snickering, Lathe murmured, "How could I not. Hmmm?"

"Of course you couldn't."

Then Holden slid his hand to Lathe's crotch and showed him a whole new reason why waking with him was so much better than a friend.

The sound of knocking coming from nearby pulled Lathe out of his post-coital bliss. Hearing Holden grumble under his breath, he groaned and eased away from his gargoyle. He settled his feet on the ground, but when he tried to stand, his left leg tightened.

Lathe would have buckled if Holden hadn't caught him.

"Easy, Lathe," Holden rumbled, his arm securely around his waist even though he was sitting. "You okay?"

Grimacing, Lathe nodded. "Yeah. Sorry." Feeling like an idiot, he rested his hand on Holden's shoulder as he stretched his leg out in front of him. "Between the cold and staying in one position for so long, guess I stiffened up."

Really, Lathe knew better than that. Spending too much time in the cold always meant he needed to warm up his knee and stretch. He'd totally neglected his health in favor of cuddling.

*Oops.*

"Why don't you hop into the shower and get cleaned up," Holden encouraged. "I'll see who's at the door and join you as quickly as I can."

Lathe nodded. "Thanks. I could really use it to loosen up my thigh muscle."

"Sorry to keep you in the cold so long," Holden murmured as he rose to his feet. "Hang on."

Before Lathe could say a word, Holden swung him up into

his arms. He wrapped his arms around his lover's neck and just went with it. Cuddled in his big gargoyle's arms, Lathe felt so cherished, and he didn't mind one bit.

When the knock came from the front of the suite again, Holden rolled his eyes and picked up his pace. "Bet that vampire enforcer is here. It's probably someone looking for you," he grumbled. Smirking, he winked and added, "I think I made you forget your phone and laptop in the front room."

Lathe grinned. "Wow. Can't remember the last time that happened."

Holden waggled his eyebrows as he stated, "Well, then I think I did my job well enough last night." He lowered him to the floor in the bathroom. "Be back in a few."

Grinning at his beloved, Lathe stated, "I can't wait."

Dipping his head, Holden captured Lathe's mouth. Unfortunately, with the continued knocking, it was short-lived. He lifted his head, breaking the kiss on a disgruntled groan.

Lathe laughed and smacked his ass. "Go get rid of them." With a wink, he began using the counter on the left to limp toward the shower. "Tell them we'll be down in twenty or something." Then he smirked and winked, doing his best to wiggle his ass while standing on one leg. "After all, it *is* your day off."

"Love your minx side," Holden rumbled, palming and fondling his ass for a few seconds before slipping from the bathroom.

Grinning, Lathe focused on getting into the shower. He couldn't remember the last time he'd had such an enjoyable evening. Of course, a major part of that was due to the kind, patient, amazing gargoyle that had just left.

"Gods, I have it bad," Lathe mumbled as he turned on the water. He stood outside the shower, waiting for the water to heat for a moment. Lathe had just stuck his arm in and decided it had warmed enough when he heard the door behind him shut. Without looking, a wide smile curving his lips, Lathe stated, "That was fast. Is everything okay?"

"Everything is perfect," a masculine tenor stated darkly. "Even better seeing you like this."

Fear slid through his veins like ice water as Lathe pivoted. Upon seeing Edward in the bathroom, he opened his mouth to scream.

Too bad Edward moved so fast, wrapping a clawed hand around Lathe's throat and stopping his air. Staring into the other vampire's malice-filled, dirt-brown eyes, Lathe vowed to make him pay the first chance he got.

Then Lathe lost consciousness.

Pain radiated through every inch of Lathe's body, rousing him from a rather pleasant dream.

*Wait. That's not just pain. That's cold.*

Keeping his breathing as even as possible, Lathe tried to remember what the hell had happened. It came back quickly enough. Somehow, Edward had managed to get into Holden's second-floor bathroom and take him . . . wherever he was.

*I'm so going to kick Raymond's ass.*

Evidently, the Falias clutch had a gap in their security that none of them had seen.

*Okay. Okay. Not the little gargoyle's fault.*

"I know you're awake."

Lathe managed to keep his body relaxed and unrespon-sive . . . until he felt a hand glide down his ass cheek. Rolling left away from the contact, he blinked quickly as he peered around. He was sort of sorry that he had.

The room betrayed its age with a single, dusty, cracked window that was reinforced with metal latticework — *no exit there.* The walls were wood and scarred with age. The flooring was just as beat up.

Lathe had been lying on a tattered mattress, and the only

other piece of furniture was the low stool Edward sat upon. The large vampire smirked at him as he rose to his full height. Peering at him imperiously, he swept his gaze over him boldly.

Lathe barely resisted the urge to cover himself. Instead, he channeled his inner mantra — *acquiring courage, acquiring courage* — and stood to his full height. He even tipped his chin up and stared straight back at the other male. No way was he going to be cowed by this bastard again.

"You've picked up some bad habits while I was away, pet," Edward stated coldly, his cruelty bleeding through in his voice. "You'd do well not to anger me." His eyes narrowed, and he swept his gaze over Lathe's body again. "Especially since I do enjoy looking at you so, and it's so very cold at night." Then Edward's gaze fell to the scarring over the left side of his body, and his lip curled in disgust. "Although, maybe I should give you some boxers to hide those unsightly scars."

"These are your fault," Lathe stated boldly. "You caused them."

Snorting, Edward rolled his eyes. "This may come as a shock, but I didn't start that fire." With a negligent shrug, he told him, "I was out buying bandages for your leg when it started."

While that was one answer to a question Lathe had wondered for many years, he responded by shrugging one shoulder. "And you were the one who did this to my leg, rendering me unconscious, so, eh, still your fault."

Lathe continued to hold Edward's gaze as he waited for the vampire's next taunt. Plus, there was no way he wanted to turn his back on the dangerous male. From the way so little light filtered in through the broken window, he knew that night had fallen. He must have been missing for a while. That meant he just had to bide his time.

*My beloved will be looking for me. He'll find me.*

Lathe held onto that thought with every fiber of his being.

"Well, get comfortable," Edward stated, waving negligently at the tattered futon. "I'll bring you some water later . . . if I think of it."

That had been a common threat, too.

*Be good or you'll go hungry . . . or thirsty . . . or be abused.*

Lathe didn't respond as he watched Edward leave the room. He heard a heavy padlock click into place, telling him that there was most likely no way out that way. He turned his attention to the window.

Ever so carefully — he didn't need a splinter — Lathe made his way over to the window. True to what Edward had threatened, cold air swooped in through the cracks. Inhaling deeply, Lathe took in the scents outside.

*Huh. That's not the only thing that's seeping in through the slats. I know that smell, and I don't mean the pine.*

It hit him. Tasker's arousal.

*Oh, fucking hell. Was the gargoyle out there fucking?*

Grimacing, Lathe knew he had to take the chance. "Tasker," he hissed.

For several seconds, he heard nothing. Then a soft moan carried on the breeze. The ever-so-quiet slap of flesh on flesh reached Lathe's ears.

Rubbing his weak thigh on reflex, Lathe wanted to scream. Instead, he waited . . . and waited . . . and waited some more.

*Good grief. Just how long could the asshole go?*

Finally, the low grunts of completion reached Lathe's ears, telling them that Tasker had finished fucking . . . whoever. He barely resisted banging his head against the glass as he counted to ten. Then he could wait no longer.

"Tasker," Lathe snarled softly with a glance toward the door. "Pay attention, goddamnit. It's Lathe, and I need help."

"Who the hell is that?" A soft male voice sounded concerned.

Tasker answered a little too loudly. "Lathe? What the hell

are you doing out here?"

"Keep your voice down and come here," Lathe demanded.

Tasker muttered something to his . . . fuck-buddy, then spoke a little louder. "Where the hell are you?"

"Um, follow the sound of my voice?" Lathe guessed. "You'll run into a cabin eventually."

"A cabin," Tasker grumbled, sounding annoyed. "The only cabin out here is supposed to be Grimley's."

"I don't know anything about someone named Grimley," Lathe admitted, frowning. "I just know I'm locked up in here."

To Lathe's shock, he saw a coal-black eye peer in through a crack in the glass. Jerking back, he barely resisted squeaking in alarm. He gaped as he watched that black eye blink an eyelid just as dark.

"You said you're locked up in there?" a deep dark voice asked.

"Yes," Lathe answered on instinct.

A dangerous-sounding growl filled the air. "By who?"

"E-Edward," Lathe replied softly, easing back toward the window. "He's been stalking me. Attacked me a few years back."

A malicious snarl almost drowned out the sound of the lock on the door being opened.

"Oh, gods," Lathe whispered, turned to face Edward. "He's coming."

"Stay by the window," the man with the dark voice and black eyes ordered.

Deciding to take the devil he didn't know, Lathe stood by the window.

"Who are you talking to?" Edward demanded.

Lathe didn't answer. Instead, he stared at the man defiantly and waited.

"I asked you a question, pet." Edward stalked toward him,

and it took everything in Lathe to stay still. "Tell me now."

Taking one step to the side drew Edward close to the window. Evidently, that was what . . . whoever . . . had been waiting for. Glass and metal shattered, erupting inward. A black-clawed hand reached through the window casing, grabbed Edward, and hauled him through the gaping space.

In the next instant, a scream rent the air.

Lathe took a step backward, only to wince when he felt glass cut into his foot. To his shock, Tasker's blue frame appeared. He glanced around the room before focusing on Lathe.

"Come on," Tasker beckoned, reaching through the opening. "Let's get you back to Holden. I called him after I heard your voice, and he's frantic."

Limping close to the window, Lathe stared at the jagged glass filling the window.

Shrugging, Tasker lifted his loincloth, wrapped it around his hand, and swiped it over the frame, clearing it of glass shards.

Groaning, Lathe accepted the male's hand and allowed himself to be lifted free. As he swung out of the building, a chill went through him as he took in the scene.

The biggest gargoyle he'd ever seen stood amidst the trees. He was black as night, appearing more shadow than form. His eyes reflected the meager moonlight that reached the forest floor.

Blood sprayed across the nearby tree trunks, and Edward's clearly shredded body littered the forest floor.

Even as a shiver of fear slithered through him, Lathe managed to find his tongue. "Thank you," he called. As Lathe was lifted into Tasker's arms and hurried away, he looked over the blue gargoyle's shoulder, staring back at the other male. The gargoyle lifted a hand, and Lathe felt certain he heard the male's deep, rumbly voice call, "You're welcome."

*So that's Grimley.*

# EPILOGUE

Holden had wanted to pull out his hair more than once over the last few hours. He was certain he'd experienced the longest twelve hours of his life.

After telling Enforcer Einan that he and Lathe would be to Chieftain Maelgwn's study within half an hour, he'd headed to the shower . . . only to find it empty. The French doors had been open, and a strange scent had been in his room. Holden had immediately given chase, but he'd lost the trail amidst the trees.

He hated to admit it, but he wasn't much of a tracker.

Instead, Holden had needed to call Einan back and share the situation.

After Holden had been pacing for an hour, Raymond had discovered the malware that had caused one of their southern boundary security cameras to show a loop of footage. They'd never even suspected that someone had snuck onto their property. Half a dozen trackers had been dispatched.

Imagine Holden's surprise to overhear a phone call that Tasker had made to Chieftain Maelgwn. It had been dumb luck that the other gargoyle had decided to take Beldrew out there to have a screw. Still, as odd as it was, Holden would be forever grateful.

Tasker had enlisted the help of the reclusive Grimley, and they'd rescued Lathe.

Holden couldn't wait to have his mate back in his arms. Of course, he was a little unnerved to share that the reason the

Vampire Enforcer had reported Edward dead had been because he'd been paid off. Fortunately, that bastard was dead, double-crossed by Edward.

*Couldn't have happened to a nicer guy.*

Movement between the trees drew Holden's attention. He watched Tasker appear, holding Lathe. With a growl, he realized the blue gargoyle was naked.

"The male has no shame," Chieftain Maelgwn grumbled, shaking his head.

Holden silently agreed, but he was too busy calling, "Lathe," and running to meet him. "Just had to show him your dick again," Holden grumbled, taking his mate from Tasker.

Tasker waggled his brows and teased, "I'm not the only one naked."

Feeling Lathe's naked flesh, Holden finally recognized the truth. His mate was also nude. "Shit." He met Lathe's deep green eyes. "Are you okay?"

Lathe smiled up at him and cuddled into Holden's embrace. "I'm good," he assured. "Really." Petting Holden's pectoral, he assured, "Your clutch-mates stopped Edward before he could do anything. Permanently."

"Good. Do you need a doctor?" Holden really just wanted to secret his mate away for . . . the foreseeable future, but if he was hurt—

"No. I'm not hurt," Lathe assured. "Had a bit of glass in my foot, but Tasker removed it on our way back." Rubbing his palms over Holden's chest, he soothed, "I'm already healed."

"Okay." Holden spread his wings as he called to his chieftain. "I need twenty-four hours."

"Hell," Chieftain Kinsey called back. "Take forty-eight."

Chieftain Maelgwn nodded, his expression solemn.

"Thank you." Then Holden beat his wings and took to the air. As he flew to his balcony, he stated, "This time, I'm going to shower with you."

Lathe smiled up at him. "Good. I'd really like that."

"Forever," Holden declared.

Nodding again, Lathe repeated, "Forever."

As Holden took them to the bathroom, he heard Lathe say, "So, uh, I'd like to officially meet Grimley. I'd like to thank him."

"He's not really a people person," Holden warned as he reached into the shower to turn on the water.

Lathe nodded slowly, then offered him a mischievous grin. "You think I should just send him a gift basket?"

Holden bit back a scoff even as he nodded, too, all the while wondering what kind of gift basket Grimley would even like.

Regardless, Holden knew his life with Lathe would never be boring, and he looked forward to every minute of it.

# About the Author

Charlie started writing fantasy when she was eight, and after stumbling onto her first erotic romance at age nineteen, she realized her true calling. She now focuses on writing gay erotic romance, normally of the paranormal variety, with heroes of all kinds. With the help and support of her husband, Charlie finally fulfilled one of her life-long goals . . . move to acreage with her horses. You can often find her curled up with her laptop and a cup of tea or glass of wine, creating her next adventure. Charlie enjoys exploring the mountains of her new Oregon home on horseback, 4-wheeler, or motorcycle.

She can be reached at ch.richards2010@yahoo.com

Or visit her at www.charlie-richards.com.